The·Merry·

Adventures·of,

Robin·Hood:

The·Merry·Friar·carrieth· Robin·across·the·Water :·

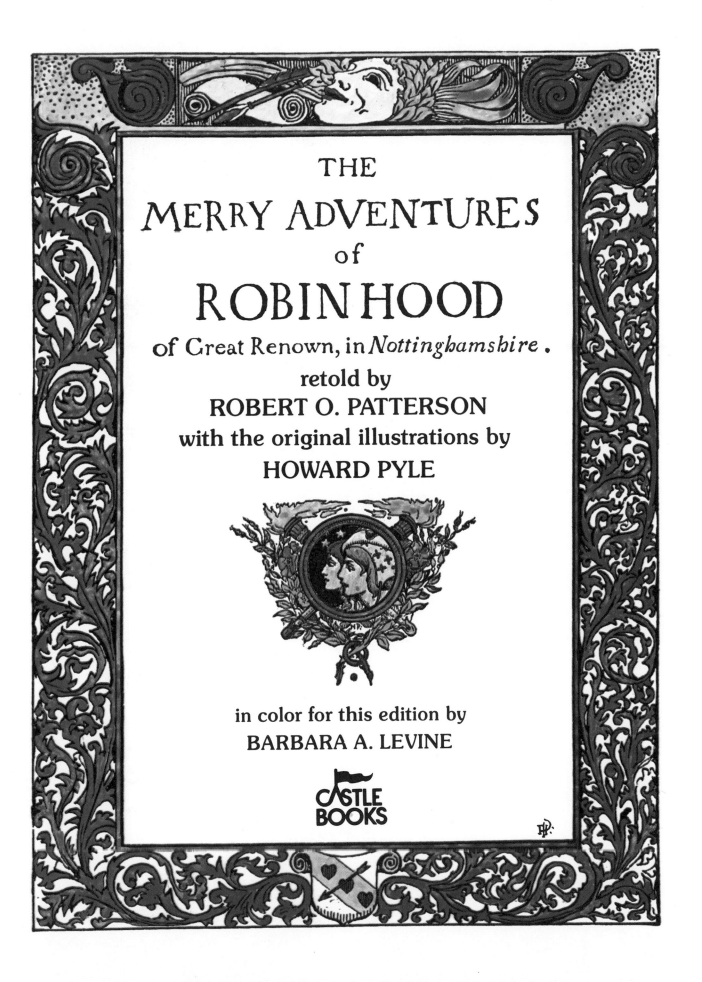

THE
MERRY ADVENTURES
of
ROBIN HOOD

of Great Renown, in *Nottinghamshire*.

retold by

ROBERT O. PATTERSON

with the original illustrations by

HOWARD PYLE

in color for this edition by

BARBARA A. LEVINE

CASTLE
BOOKS

Manufactured in the United States of America.

ISBN NO.: 0-89009-388-1

PREFACE

CHAPTER ONE

CHAPTER TWO

CHAPTER THREE

CHAPTER FOUR

CHAPTER FIVE

CHAPTER SIX

CHAPTER SEVEN

CHAPTER EIGHT

CHAPTER NINE

The Merry Adventures of Robin Hood:

Robin Hood Grows Up In Nottinghamshire

I n the fertile midlands of England, in the small village of Locksley, in the county of Nottingham, in the eleventh year of the reign of King Henry II, a son was born to Sir William and Ada Fitzooth. Robert Fitzooth was born in the summertime. He was so fair and sunburned so easily that his nurse made him a little cape with a big hood to shield his face from the sun. Seeing the little baby hidden inside such a large hood, his father laughed and called him "Robin Hood." Soon, everyone was calling him that.

Robin's father, Sir William, had, long before, been Earl of Huntingdon, but he was forced out of his vast lands and had his title taken away when King Henry came to power. Now he had only a small farm estate in Nottingham county. His manor had to support not only Sir William and his family, but the families of 25 farm workers.

When Robin was four, the manor priest began to teach him how to read and write, first in Latin, the language of the church, then in French, the language of the King and nobles, and then in English, the language of the common people.

In the fall of Robin's ninth year, a fever struck the manor village. Robin's mother became sick. Sir William brought famous doctors from as far away as London town, but nothing they did seemed to help her. Slowly, quietly, his mother became weaker, until one morning she didn't awaken. Robin was heartbroken, for he had loved his mother very dearly.

His older sister Alice came home for several weeks from Maxwell, where she lived with her husband, Sir Rolph Scarlock. She tried to comfort Robin, but he felt like his heart was broken.

Robin didn't know his father had spent all of the family's money trying to make Robin's mother well. He had been forced to borrow money from the Bishop of York and pledge his land as security for the loan. If Sir William failed to make the payment, the Bishop would take the land away from him.

Robin Learns The Manly Arts Of Battle

One morning, as he started across the manor yard, he was stopped by a familiar call.

"Hold there, Robin, I wish to talk to you." It was his father. He put his hand on the boy's shoulder.

"I hadn't realized how big you've grown. It's about time your education takes a turn for more useful, manly pursuits." Robin's heart fell; it sounded like more school.

"Stutely, come here a moment," Sir William called to his elderly bailiff, John Stutely, who helped him on the estate. "I think it's high time that Robert here, who is ten, should be given training in archery. What would you say to your son Will showing him how to shoot a bow?"

The older man grinned and said, "He should be able to show the young master how to start, milord." He turned and whistled shrilly.

Robin's heart leaped with joy. Will Stutely was

9

six years older, and Robin had often watched him shoot at the archery targets.

The English archer was said to be the best in the world. The finest archers could hit a target at a quarter of a mile away, and the long bows, nearly as tall as a man, could send the yard-long arrows through a thick piece of oak at fifty yards. Almost every able bodied man was expected to be able to shoot a bow accurately when he was called up for army duty. Training to be an archer started early, with fathers teaching sons.

Within seconds, the Stutely boy was trotting around the end of the stable. "You called, father?" he asked.

"I'm going to give you a little rest from work, Will," his father said. "Sir William here wants young Robin to learn how to shoot a bow. Find him one he can handle and show him how to shoot."

The two boys were soon trotting away. Robin's father turned back to the bailiff. "I'll break away from work an hour each day and teach the boy how to handle a sword. He must learn how to defend himself."

Will Stutely made Robin a bow of strong, springy wood from the yew tree and taught him how to shoot it straight and true. And every day, Sir William spent an hour teaching swordplay to the boy. Both sports built Robin's arms and shoulders quickly.

Robin was a natural athlete and soon was able to shoot a bow like a soldier and use a sword like a knight. On his own, Will started teaching Robin how to fight with a quarterstaff, a long pole with which the farmers fought in contests during the summer.

Time seemed to pass like lightning for Robin. The months grew into years and the friendship between the two boys grew stronger each year. They spent more and more time in nearby Sherwood Forest, where Will knew all the trails. They had a favorite place, a large clearing in the heart of the forest, far from people, where they would play at being foresters and practice their archery.

By the time Robin was 18, he had reached his full growth and was a tall, muscular young man who could beat Will Stutely at quarterstaves, often beat his father at swordplay, and could hit the target with his arrows better than any man in the village.

CHAPTER 1

Robin Hood Comes To Sherwood Forest To Live

n April of his 18th year, Robin heard about the archery contest to be given on May 1 by the Sheriff of Nottingham. On the May Day holiday, the Sheriff always had a contest, but the prize that year was very large. It was to be a purse of five pounds gold for the very best archer. That was just the amount of money Robin needed to pay on the Bishop of York's loan.

Robin decided to enter the contest. His father had become very old. Finally, the elder Fitzooth became ill, and he lay in bed at a time when he was needed to supervise the planting of the year's crops.

On the morning of May Day, Robin rose as usual at 5:00 a.m. and quickly stole away from the manor house with the things he had made ready the night before.

He was dressed in a suit of Lincoln green. Over his shoulder he had a pouch with some bread and cheese and three copper pennies, which was all the money he had in the world. He also had his bow and arrows, a quarterstaff and a sharp sword.

The shortest way to Nottingham town was through Sherwood Forest, and Robin knew the way well. Therefore, he wasn't paying much atten-tion when he walked into a group of six men around a small fire in the woods.

"Ho," said the biggest one, who had a full black beard. "What's this young, smooth-faced boy doing in the King's forest? And dressed like a King's forester, too."

Robin saw they were all dressed in green, also. They must be the new foresters which the Sheriff of Nottingham had hired to stop people who were shooting and trapping deer, hare and pheasant as times got harder.

"I'm on my way to the archery contest," Robin said proudly.

"Are you now?" The leader laughed. "Do you think a young pipsqueak like you will have any chance against the best archers in Nottingham-shire?"

"I can beat even Will Stutely," Robin said firmly.

"Whoever this Will Stutely is, then, he can't be much," the forester said. "I'm going to enter the contest, and I'm the best bowman in the county." His fellows agreed loudly.

"I don't care," Robin said. "I need the money, and I'm going to win."

"If you're so good," the forester said, getting up and stringing a bow, "you might want to have a small contest with me. What say you to a bet of two coppers?"

Robin laid down his quarterstaff and pouch and strung his bow. "All right. Shall we shoot at a tree or set up a wand?" he asked.

"Let's make it interesting. See that herd of deer at the end of the glade? I bet you can't hit that big hart."

Robin pulled out an arrow and let it fly. The big hart took one startled bound into the air and fell with the shaft half buried behind its front shoulder.

"You owe me two pennies," Robin said proudly.

"I owe you an arrest for killing the King's deer," snarled the angry head forester. "That's a hanging offense."

The boy suddenly remembered King Henry's Forest Law, which decreed death for killing deer in a King's forest.

"But you picked the target," Robin said heatedly.

"So much a fool you are, then," the forester said with an ugly laugh. "You're under arrest!"

Scared, Robin scooped up his pouch and quarterstaff and ran for the woods. As he ran, an arrow whistled by his ear. He stopped and turned to see the head forester reaching for another arrow.

Robin dropped pouch and quarterstaff and swiftly shot an arrow, striking the forester in the shoulder. As the bearded man fell with a cry, the other foresters ran for their weapons. Once again, Robin grabbed his possessions and ran headlong into Sherwood Forest, knowing that he was now an outlaw.

Robin Builds His Band Of Merry Men

For three days Robin hid in the forest. Occasionally he heard voices, and he knew he was being hunted.

Robin ate all his bread and cheese the first day, but managed to trap at least one hare a day, so he was well fed. But he worried. He wanted to get word to his father, but he knew the Sheriff's men would go to the manor at once. While he hunted, he unconsciously worked his way toward the center of the forest and the large glade where he and Will Stutely had spent so many happy hours.

Cautious now, Robin approached the big clearing warily. He was surprised to see several men sitting on the moss beside the little stream. Most of them were tattered and dirty, and he was amazed to see one was Will Stutely, his best friend.

Will, with the hearing of a cat, shouted, "Whoever you are, step forth and identify yourself. We're peaceful men and don't like to be spied upon."

Robin stepped from the trees, to find himself the target of seven drawn bows, which had appeared like magic in their hands.

"Robin," Will shouted. "I was hoping you'd find your way back here!"

The two friends ran together and pounded each other's backs. The other six men lowered their weapons.

With his arm around Robin's shoulders, Will turned to the group, "Men, this is the very Robin Hood I've been telling you about. The best archer, the best wrestler, the best swordsman, the best with a quarterstaff in the county."

As the other six inspected Robin carefully, Will said, "I bear bad news, I fear. Your father, told about your ill fortune by the Sheriff's men, tried to leap from bed, and his heart failed. He is dead, Robin."

Robin tried to pull away from his friend's arm. "I must go back to the manor."

"I'm afraid not, Robin," Will said. "The moment your father died, the Sheriff's men notified the Bishop, and they are now dividing up everything. There is nothing to go back for."

"But surely you can get some of our personal things," Robin said.

Will shook his head. "I'm afraid not. When those villains crowded into your father's room and caused his death, I went wild and knocked the heads of three of them and ran. I'm afraid I'm a fugitive now, too.

"But come meet your fellow outlaws, Robin. These are all good men who have been wandering in Sherwood. I found them as I hunted you.

"This mighty young giant is David of Doncaster. He is reckoned the best wrestler in the Midlands. His master died this winter past, and David had to kill a deer to eat." The two men clasped hands.

"This is John Sparrow, accused of trapping birds

to feed his starving family. And this is Ralph of Wakefield, a cobbler's apprentice who could not stand the beatings his master gave him. Adam the Fletcher here once made winning arrows for the great Adam Bell himself, yet he was foreclosed from his shop by the abbot of St. Mary's.

"And this tall, lean scarecrow is Clyde de Morrow. A freeman, he had his papers stolen by a Sheriff's constable. He can read and cypher like a very clerk of the abbey."

Will turned to the last one, a short, fat man of middle years. His bald head looked like the shaved head of a friar. "And this is Simeon of York. Sim is — by his own account — the best cook of venison in England, and the King wants to meet him — at the end of a rope. You are just an amateur deer slayer compared to him. How many have you killed, Sim?"

The older outlaw smiled gently. "By my reckoning, it stands at 24 over the past six years. And were I a better bowman, 'twould have been double that."

Robin Wrestles David Of Doncaster And Makes Plans

Robin saw David of Doncaster was watching him eagerly.

"Will called you a good wrestler," David said. "Would you like to give me a fall or two?"

Will said, "This young hulk has bested some of the finest wrestlers in the Midlands. They say he has never taken a fall."

That caught Robin's curiosity. "Never a fall? Is this true, Doncaster?"

"As I stand here, I have never been given a fall by any man." The redhead grinned. "Are you willing to let me knock you about a bit to prove the point?"

"Aye," Robin said. "I'll take you on, two falls out of three."

Warily, the two men stepped toward each other. Suddenly, David darted forward, caught Robin around the arms and body, and threw him to the ground. The men cheered.

"First fall to David," Will shouted. "Get up, Robin, and have at it again."

Robin slowly rose to his feet. He realized David was quick and wily. Robin determined to use a trick Will had shown him.

Again, they advanced toward each other. Robin, as if afraid, took a quick step backwards. David rushed in. He made another grab at Robin.

Robin quickly pivoted to one side, thrust out a hip and grabbed David's arm, pulling the wrestler forward. David shot into the air and ended in a somersault, landing on his back with the wind driven out of him. The others cheered Robin.

"Second fall to Robin," Will yelled. "Come on, David, your perfect record is gone, so see if you can keep Robin from winning."

David came slowly to his feet and looked at Robin in wonder. "You're the first man who has ever gotten me off my feet," he said. "You must teach me that fall when the match is over."

Both men now circled warily. Each made feints at the other. The other men yelled encouragement, now for one, now for the other.

All at once, David came forward in a fast lunge, to hit Robin in the stomach. As Robin felt himself falling, he grabbed David's long red hair and pulled him over, too. Both men fell, with David doing another somersault, to end up lying on his back, head to head with Robin. They were both stunned by the fall.

Will shouted, laughing, "Two falls out of three for each one. I declare a tie for the two best wrestlers in the Midlands!" He helped them to their feet.

With laughing and back slapping, the two were surrounded by the others. The wrestlers looked at each other and smiled.

"That was the best match I've had since I started beating old Will here," Robin said, gasping for breath.

"For me as well," David said, panting. "Thrown not only once, but twice. I swear I'll cut this hair so short no one else will ever get such a grip on it."

When the laughing had died down, Robin looked at the little band of outcasts.

"Men, if we are outlaws, then we must make the best of it. Let's organize so we are no longer at the mercy of the Sheriff and the elements."

Robin had naturally assumed the role of leader, and the others gathered to hear what he would say.

Robin Hood Makes His Rules And All Agree

Robin said, "We must have some rules. None of us are bad men, but we have broken the King's laws, and if we are caught, the Sheriff, acting for the King, will surely hang us, one and all." Everyone nodded.

"I propose these rules," Robin said. "We shall never take anything from a common man. We shall help those who need help. We shall live by taking away the ill gotten gains of the rich and greedy. We shall share our money with common people who are in need. We will never harm or threaten a woman, and we shall always behave as true men."

Robin paused to think. "And, most important, we must never admit to our band any murderer, liar or cheat." The men murmured agreement.

Robin said, "We have many of the skills which we're going to need to live here in Sherwood Forest. Will, you know the forest best. Maybe you can find others who are sheltering here who will fit into our band.

"John Sparrow, you are a hunter. You can supply Simeon with meat to cook. Adam, you must make the arrows we'll need to hunt deer and defend ourselves from the Sheriff's men.

"Clyde, you shall be our treasurer and keep track of our supplies. David, besides a wrestler, you look like a farmer."

The young man smiled. "The best in the Earl of Doncaster's demesne."

"And what about me?" Ralph of Wakefield asked.

Robin said, "You must be our cobbler, but we must still find someone to clothe us."

"That's not hard," Ralph said. "I have a trick with the needle and can even make my own clothes."

"Good, we must be dressed well, not only to protect ourselves from the elements, but from the Sheriff's men," Robin said. "So I propose we all dress alike in Lincoln green. It fades into the woods and will make us look like King's foresters from a distance. We must not look like vagabonds and outcasts."

Will asked, "And what part will you play in our little band, Robin?"

"I shall be the moneyer, and shall mint good gold and silver coin from the purses of the wealthy." Robin laughed. "If outlaws we must be, let us earn the reputation."

Robin Meets John Little And They Fight

With everyone at their tasks, Robin started for the edge of the forest to see if he could find some money, for the three pennies in his pouch were the only money they had.

He came to a strong brook, ten feet wide, and over a foot or two deep in the middle. The only place to cross was a log someone had braced there. Just as Robin bounded up on the log, he saw someone jump onto it from the other end.

"Hey, fellow," Robin called. "Step aside and let me across. I was here first."

"Step aside yourself, youngster," the big man at the other end growled. Robin saw he was at least a head taller, and Robin was a very tall man.

"If you don't step aside, I'll knock you off," Robin said angrily.

"You can try," the giant said. "If you want a dunking, I'll be glad to give it to you." He advanced with a quarterstaff held across his chest.

Robin raised his own quarterstaff and started across. They met in the middle of the log. Robin found the stranger towered over him threateningly. Suddenly, the big man thrust at Robin's legs, which Robin easily struck aside. He swung at the giant's head.

With both blows failing, each knew he had met a master. The fight then began in earnest. The cudgels rose and fell, swung around and thrust and parried. The forest rang to the blows.

Suddenly, the big stranger cracked Robin on the shin and nearly made him lose his balance. In return, Robin struck the other on his elbow, which nearly caused the man to lose his staff. Another flurry of blows.

Then Robin hit the big man's shoulder, and the giant stepped backwards to keep balance. Robin

Robin Hood · meeteth · the · tall Stranger · on · the · Bridg

leaned forward to finish the job, when he found himself struck in the stomach and rudely dropped into two feet of cold water.

Just then, Will Stutely and John Sparrow ran out of the woods. They had heard the fight from nearby. "Hold on, Robin," Will yelled. "We'll pound this lummox for you."

"No, no," Robin managed to shout. "He beat me fairly." He held up his hand and the giant reached out his staff to help Robin to his feet.

Dripping, Robin was pulled up the bank by the tall man as Will and John reached them.

"This is indeed a shrewd one with the quarterstaff," Robin said. "I was outmatched." He held

out his hand to the big man, who looked at him searchingly, then clasped it with his own.

"I am John Little, a nailer from Barnsley, and I'm looking for work at Nottingham town," he said.

"Are you a freeman, then?" Will asked.

"Aye, and my father before me, and his father before him. I go where I please, and no man dare stop me," the giant boasted.

"And I am Robin Hood, and these are Will Stutely and John Sparrow, also forest dwellers."

"Outlaws, you mean," Little John laughed. "You two look a bit ragged for successful outlaws," he said to Will and John. "But you might be interested in my story."

The Poor Widow And Her Outlaw Sons

"Not more than a mile away," John Little said, "I came to a little clearing and heard the sounds of sobbing in the rude hut there."

Will Stutely said, "That's the poor widow Jenkins' place. Her sons are still too young to work the land. They do poorly."

"You're right," John Little said. "She told me her sons had just been taken away by the Sheriff's foresters."

"Taken away for what?" Robin asked, puzzled.

"The older boy, in despair because his younger brothers were starving, killed a hind today. The new King's foresters trailed him to the hut. They caught him redhanded. They took the boys to be hanged under the Forest Law."

"Wait a minute," Robin cried. "Why did they take all three boys?"

"They found all three cutting up the deer," the big man said. "The Sheriff has sworn to hang the first deer killer caught. He's going to hold the trial at the King's Arms Inn, where he and Prince John have been hunting this week. Since you're outlaws, I thought you might like to know."

Robin turned to the other two outlaws. "He's right. We can't let this happen to three good boys whose only crime is being hungry. Let's see what we can do." He asked John Little, "Do you want to join us?"

"No, I'm a law abiding man. I'll just go on about my business."

Robin jumped up. "Thank you, John Little. You're certainly skilled with a quarterstaff. God be

with you." The three outlaws trotted away.

Back at the clearing, Robin found David, Simeon, and Clyde and told them what had happened. All three agreed they should help the widow's sons.

When the six outlaws reached the Inn, they saw the Sheriff's men were guarding the three frightened boys tied to a post. A small crowd of people were watching the "criminals." The oldest was 15 years old, and the other two were 12 and 14.

Robin said to the others, "Get to the front of the crowd. String your bows for action." Robin strode briskly up to look at the boys.

A big guard started to shoo him away. A voice called from the door of the inn, "No, let the young fellow take a look. That, my fine young man in green, is what happens to those who kill the King's deer."

Robin looked up to see a big fat man wearing fine robes and a great hat. Robin recognized the Sheriff of Nottingham. Beside him was a thin young man with a weasel face and shifty eyes. The Sheriff turned to him. "You see, Prince John, everyone is curious, but none are willing to be hangmen. Three times I've asked for volunteers. They want to see the fun, but they don't want to help."

Prince John, the youngest son of King Henry II, muttered something Robin couldn't hear. The Sheriff turned to Robin. "Young sir, would you like a silver shilling?" he asked with a greasy smile. "Just hang those three criminals."

"I wouldn't want to take that pleasure away from your own men," Robin replied.

"No, no, it's best a stranger do it," the Sheriff said.

Robin thought quickly and then nodded.

"Fine. What is your name, young sir," the Sheriff asked.

"Hobin Rood, your honor."

"Then here, Hobin, is your shilling." The Sheriff tossed a coin to Robin. "Give Hobin Rood the rope," he called to one of his men. "You may use the tree there."

Robin leaned down as if to hear what one boy was saying. He said quietly, "When I cut your bonds, run to that big man in brown there in front of the crowd. We'll get you away safe."

He straightened up and yelled, "Now, men!" Then he hit the nearest guard on the jaw, drew his dagger and cut the boys' ropes.

His men drew their bows, but so did the guards, and the frightened crowd was now in the way. Out of the corner of his eye, Robin saw Prince John spring back through the inn door and slam it, stranding the Sheriff outside.

As Robin hesitated, a great voice shouted over the cries of the crowd. "Sheriff, order your men to drop their weapons, or my first arrow will seek your fat gut!"

It was the giant John Little, standing at the corner of the inn yard with an arrow aimed at the Sheriff. The Sheriff yelled, "Don't shoot," in one breath and wildly cried for his men to drop their bows in another. The men obeyed.

Robin ran the ten steps to the Sheriff and jerked the purse from his belt. He bowed. "Thank you, sire, for a poor widow who needs this coin far more than you." Then he trotted away.

"But, Hobin Rood..." the Sheriff called after him.

Over his shoulder Robin answered, "Not Hobin Rood, but Robin Hood, Sheriff. Remember that name when you next catch a poor unfortunate."

"Come on men, bring the boys and follow me," Robin called and ran toward the corner of the inn. Once there, he joined the big man in guarding the Sheriff's men. By this time the only thing seen of the crowd was a pair of heels disappearing around the other end of the inn.

As his men pounded past, Robin grinned at John Little and said, "I think it's about time you and I left, too."

Both men shot their arrows into the dirt near the Sheriff and his guards, who all fell to the ground for safety. Robin and John then ran. Just as they entered the forest, the guards' arrows came whistling after them, but they escaped into the safety of the trees.

A Christening And The Band Grows By Five

Well into the woods, the men and boys slowed down. "You may be quite an outlaw," John Little said, looking at the Sheriff's purse which Robin carried, "but you're not much of a soldier."

"What do you mean?" Robin asked.

"When I followed to see the fun, I discovered you hadn't placed your men right and hadn't prepared an avenue of retreat," the big man said.

"You sound like you've had experience," Robin said.

"I was on King Henry's Irish campaigns three years ago, and when I was just a lad, I helped stop a raid from the Scots. I was a front rank archer," John Little said proudly.

He shook his head, sorrowfully. "But now I've become an outlaw, just because I couldn't keep my nose out of another's business." He wiped a mock tear from his eye.

Will Stutely burst out laughing. "John Little, you're misnamed. From now on, you're to be known as Little John, under the protection of Robin Hood's band of merry men." Robin and the rest laughed merrily.

When they reached the center of the forest, the other members of the band had returned. For a few minutes questions and answers were shouted back and forth. Then Will Stutely cried for silence.

"We have a new babe who needs christening," he said solemnly, "a poor child misnamed John Little, when everyone can see he should be called 'Little John.'" Before the giant could resist, hands pinned his arms to his sides.

Will pointed at bald headed Simeon. "Friar, prepare for the christening."

The cook filled his cupped hands with water. "Who gives this babe for christening?" he asked, trying to keep a straight face.

"Why I do," said Will Stutely.

"What name do you give this frolicsome child?"

"Little John, to match his size," Will said.

"Then, Little John, in hope you'll grow up to be a big, brawny lad, I hereby christen you," and Simeon dashed the handful of brook water into Little John's face.

With a sputter and a roar, Little John tried to pull free of his captors, who were afraid to let go.

"Hold there, nailer," Robin cried. "The name does indeed do you justice. But I wish to speak more seriously, so gentlemen, please let him go." The others jumped back out of harm's way.

But all John did was to wipe the water out of his eyes and beard and look at Robin. "Talk of what?"

"You've become an outcast," Robin said. "I thank you for the act which caused it, and I'd like to have you with us. We need counsel in military skills, and we'd like the comradeship of such a stalwart friend. If you join us, you shall be my right hand man and military chief. What say you?"

Little John let his eyes rove about the glade and the busy men there. Then he looked back at Robin.

"I say yes, if you'll grant two favors," he replied.

"Ask them," Robin said.

"First, the boys will be caught if they go home. If they don't, the widow will starve. I request the widow and the boys be allowed to join us here."

"Done," said Robin. "What more?"

"Second, you find some axes and hammers so I may build a house here for the widow. There is no better nailer in Nottinghamshire than I."

"That, too," Robin cried. "But one condition. You — with our help — must build houses for us all."

And so the little band grew from seven to 12. And Robin gained a loyal lieutenant who would fight beside him for many a day.

Robin Worries The Sheriff, Who Sees The King

By September, Robin's little band had grown to 40 first class fighting men, skilled with bow and sword. Several new men brought their wives and children with them into forest exile. Outlaws were increasing because the Sheriff of Nottingham was busily enforcing the harsh Forest Law of Henry II.

The band had, by their very numbers and willingness to do battle, forced the King's foresters to the outer edge of the forest. Robin sent small bands of men to the great north to south highway, Watling Street, with orders to bring back any wealthy priest, merchant, or noble that happened by.

When one had been brought to the forest glade, blindfolded so he could not tell the way, he was entertained by a lavish dinner of venison and hare and pheasant, by shows of archery and quarterstaff play, and by songs and ballads. Then the guest was courteously relieved of half of his money if he had been well behaved, all of it if he had not. Blindfolded, he was then returned to the highway.

The word quickly reached the Sheriff that the outlaws — for the first time in history — were organized and not mere outcasts who could be caught one by one. The Sheriff reasoned if he could capture and execute the leader, Robin Hood, the rest would be easily rounded up.

Therefore, he led a large raid into the forest, guided by an outlaw whom Robin had rejected from the band as being a liar and cheat. Robin's sentries quickly heard the big, noisy force approach, and it was ambushed far from the outlaws' camp. The Sheriff's brave men were soon running pellmell for home.

This was too much for the Sheriff. He decided to go to London, to see King Henry II. So with a small army of his guards, he set off for the King's palace.

The Sheriff arrived to find a festive air. The King, surrounded by hangers on and giggling women, reminded the Sheriff the good Queen Eleanor had been a prisoner at Winchester for nine years, since she had taken part in a baron's revolt against the King's harsh laws.

The King was not pleased to be interrupted in his drinking and entertainment.

"Well, Sheriff, what can I do for you? And be quick about it," the King said.

"Sire," the Sheriff replied, "I find my county ter-

The·Sheriff·of·Nottingham·cometh·before·the·King·at·London

rorized by a great outlaw, a Robin Hood, who has collected an army of the most vicious criminals in England, and slays and lays waste throughout Nottingham." The Sheriff didn't mention he could get no help from the common people, who all supported Robin.

"How many men would you say this notorious outlaw has?" the King asked, with a little smile.

"Why, at least a hundred," the Sheriff replied. "All vicious thieves and murderers, your majesty."

"You arrived with two hundred armed men," the King said quietly. Then he roared, "You call yourself a sheriff? You can't catch one outlaw who has only a hundred men while you have more than two hundred? Get out of here and hang that outlaw — or I will make someone sheriff who can!"

The Sheriff, frightened, backed quickly out of the King's presence, bowing nervously and nearly falling. When he returned to his men, he snarled and snapped at them as if they were at fault.

But on the gloomy ride back to Nottingham, the Sheriff had a brilliant idea.

Robin Goes To His Shooting Match After All

Many of Robin's men had come from nearby Barnsdale Forest. They were not known to the Sheriff of Nottingham and could go safely in and out of Nottingham.

One of these men told Robin the Sheriff had declared a festival, to be held outside the castle walls. There were to be festivities, ale booths and contests. The main contest would be an archery match, with a golden arrow as the prize for the best archer.

Robin immediately suspected that the Sheriff was laying a trap for him. He decided that he would set a trap for the Sheriff instead. He called a meeting. "We are going to celebrate our good fortune," he said. "Since we owe our very start to the good Sheriff of Nottingham, and our continued success to his failure to catch us, we're going to his festival in Nottingham!"

There was great shouting and laughter from the band. Robin said, "I intend to win the golden arrow and display it here in camp."

On the morning of the festival, people started arriving as soon as the sun came up. The stands for the spectators and the booths for the sale of ale and wine and food were all ready. Throughout the morning, more and more people came from the country around, until there were several hundreds on the field outside the town walls.

At high noon, the Sheriff and his court came out of the city walls and climbed into the shaded stand at the end of the field. A trumpeter sounded a call, and a page read out the list of events. The archery contest was to be held in midafternoon.

A golden-bearded archer dressed in faded, patched brown stood in the crowd looking at the nobles and their finery. He was struck by the sight of a girl who looked barely 18 standing beside the Sheriff. He turned to a nearby townswoman.

"Could you tell me, madam, who that young lady is with the Sheriff?" he asked politely.

The woman sniffed when she saw how ragged he was, but she loved to gossip. "She's the maid Marian FitzWater, who is visiting the Sheriff's wife. 'Tis said Prince John is much taken by her beauty."

The bearded man thanked her and pushed through the throng until he was beside the high stand. Sensing someone watching her, the maid Marian turned toward the crowd and looked at the bearded man. He grinned widely and swept off his feathered hat in a wide and sweeping bow. When he raised his eyes again, the girl was blushing furiously.

Then the crowd surged forward and the bearded man was carried away from the stand.

More than 50 men stepped forward when the archery contest started. But in less than an hour, there were only 10 left, and the bearded man in the tattered brown was one of them.

Some of the finest archers in the country were among those 10, including the Sheriff's chief archer, Bran Moor, and old Adam Bell, once the greatest bowman in all England.

In the stands, the Sheriff was conferring with the little nervous man who had guided the raid into Sherwood Forest. "Do you see Robin Hood or any of his men?" the Sheriff asked.

"No, sire," the little man replied. "I know only Robin Hood, Little John and Will Stutely. They blindfolded me the time they brought me to their camp. I saw none of the rest."

"Are you sure that tattered bowman isn't one of them?" the Sheriff insisted.

"Robin Hood is a beardless youth, sire, and that is an older man."

The next round eliminated five more archers. The judges then decreed that each would shoot one arrow, with the poorest shot eliminated. Finally it was down to three, the bearded stranger, Adam Bell and the Sheriff's man.

The bearded man, standing nearest to the Sheriff's stand, turned and bowed with his sweeping gesture. The Sheriff, thinking that the honor was for him, smiled and waved casually. Maid Marian blushed and dropped her eyes, which had been following the stranger.

Adam Bell shot next, his arrow hitting the target dead center. The Sheriff's man put his arrow outside the circle, to the Sheriff's great disgust. The stranger, without apparent aim, drew his bow and fired in one motion. His arrow hit Adam's squarely and splintered the shaft before thudding into the target beside it.

"That's enough for me," Adam Bell said, unstringing his bow. "Thirty-five years of shooting, but I'll not win against an aim like that."

The crowd was wildly cheering and surged forward, hiding the contestants and judges from the Sheriff's view.

"Clear the field," he shouted at his guards nearby, and they waded into the crowd.

The spectators were thickest around the bearded stranger who had won the match. Then this entire group moved together toward the stand and surrounded it.

With an agile leap from the ground, the stranger caught hold of the front railing of the stand, swung himself over it and stood, sword held lightly pointed at the Sheriff's fat stomach. Everyone in the stand rose in panic, although the maid Marian stood looking steadfastly at the intruder as two more men climbed into the stand.

"I'll take my golden arrow now, sire," the stranger said softly, and the Sheriff nervously handed it to him. "Thank you kindly, and now my friends will pass among you to accept your generous donations for the poor."

"I have no purse," the young maid said haughtily, staring directly into the stranger's eyes.

"I would not think of robbing women," replied the stranger. Then stepping close, he bent down and kissed her full on the lips. "But I will steal a kiss from such a beautiful damsel."

Then he and the other two jumped down from the stand and ran with the mob toward the woods. The Sheriff pounded his hands in frustration against the front rail of the stand and shouted to his guards. But they couldn't hear over the noise of the crowd.

On the stand, the maid Marian stood with a tiny smile on her lips, watching the stranger trotting away. On the ground below, old Adam Bell stood looking thoughtfully after a man running with the stranger.

"Hmm," Adam Bell muttered, "it seems that Adam the Fletcher has a new champion to craft true arrows for." The old man smiled and pushed through the crowd toward the ale booth.

That night, at supper, an arrow flew through a high window in the great wall of the Sheriff's castle, falling to the courtyard. A guard brought it to his captain, who brought it to the steward, who brought it to the Sheriff. Around the shaft was a parchment which said, "Thank you for the arrow, Sheriff, and thank your party for their generous contributions to the needy. Yours sincerely, Robin Hood."

Little John and Will Stutely had crept up to the walls of the castle to deliver the message. They said the Sheriff's roar of rage could be heard almost back to the glade in the middle of Sherwood Forest.

The·Sheriff·of·*Nottingham*·plotting·against·Robin·sends·a·messinger·to·L*incoln*:·

CHAPTER 2

The Sheriff Turns To Outside Help To Catch Robin

Now it would take strong measures to capture Robin Hood, the Sheriff realized. The day after the festival, he announced a bounty on Robin's head of 100 golden crowns to any man who brought him in for the Sheriff's justice.

A week later, not one person had come forward to take up the offer, even though the Sheriff had sent messengers to all the surrounding villages and towns. The Sheriff, a cunning and shrewd man, realized that Robin had endeared himself to everyone by helping the poor. So he sent a messenger to Lincoln town to find a man who would not know of Robin.

The Sheriff's man stood in Lincoln's town square and called out the King's warrant prepared by the Sheriff. A brawny tinker, heavily muscled from pounding upon pots and pans, stepped forward first. The Sheriff's messenger looked him over with approval, for the tinker looked tough.

"How are you called, tinker?" the messenger asked.

"Watny the Saxon," the tinker replied.

"Are you skilled in weapons?"

"I am the best quarterstaff man in all Lincoln," the tinker said proudly. The crowd around him murmured their agreement.

"Then, good luck with your hunt," the messenger said and handed over the warrant. Watny

took the parchment with its official looking red seal and placed it in his purse.

"How am I to get to Nottingham?" he asked.

The messenger said, "On shank's mare," then climbed into his saddle and rode away laughing.

A week later, a very weary tinker arrived at the Blue Boar Inn which stood at the edge of Sherwood. It was a pleasant fall day with the leaves turning to orange and red. The tinker decided to rest and drink a cool ale or two.

At the inn were some foresters, dressed in Lincoln green, chatting idly. They looked up as the dusty tinker entered the inn yard. The huge leader of the foresters greeted him. "You have traveled far, tinker. Sit and have an ale on us."

"With great thanks," the tinker replied. The innkeeper came out with a foaming mug of ale which the tinker drank.

"Ah," he sighed, "I needed that. I have come afoot from Lincoln, for I have most pressing business here in Nottingham."

The big forester looked interested. "Pressing business?"

"Aye, I have a warrant from the King himself for that notorious outlaw of Sherwood Forest, Robin Hood."

The big man's eyes widened. "You're going to arrest Robin Hood?" he asked with surprise.

"Yes. I need the money, and it will bring me 100 gold crowns. Where can I find this outlaw?"

The forester shook his head. "You don't find

Robin Hood. Walk in his forest and he'll find you. Do you have the skill to capture this terrible outlaw?"

"I'm the best quarterstaff fighter in Lincoln," the tinker boasted. "I intend to crack his head and bind him before he knows what's happened to him."

The large forester rose. "I wish you luck, tinker. Meanwhile, we must be on our way."

Robin Fights The Tinker With A Faulty Staff

The green-clad outlaws led by Little John immediately sought out Robin Hood.

"Robin," the big outlaw said, "the Sheriff has finally found someone to serve the warrant on you. We met a tinker from Lincoln who is determined to bring you to justice."

"Did you see the warrant?" Robin asked.

"No, but he knew there were 100 gold crowns on your head."

"I think I'll take a look at his warrant," Robin said. "I've never seen a piece of parchment worth 100 crowns. Little John, take your men and loiter near the inn within call."

Before he reached the inn, Robin could hear the tinker, forcing through the undergrowth. Robin crept up behind him.

"Ho there, stranger," Robin shouted. "What are you doing in this King's forest?"

The tinker, startled, spun about and raised his quarterstaff. Then he saw what he thought was another forester and dropped his guard. "You scared me," he admitted. "I thought you might be that outlaw, Robin Hood."

"That's a great relief, then," Robin said. "But one of my fellows said you have a warrant for the outlaw. I'd like to see it."

"I'm sorry, but I will show it only to Robin Hood himself," the tinker said.

"Then you must show it to me," Robin said, smiling. "I'm that fierce outlaw."

The tinker laughed heartily. "Stop joking, lad. I laugh so hard you'll make me cry."

Robin became irritated. "Laugh, but I'm still Robin Hood, and if you don't let me see that warrant, I'll crack your head."

The tinker stopped laughing. "You might be an outlaw at that, threatening a lawful man with a thumping. Come, then, and take it from me."

Robin raised his staff, stepped close and swung at the tinker, who blocked the bow and swung one of his own. Back and forth the two kept it up for ten minutes or more, and not one blow landed on either one.

Both were panting when, suddenly, the tinker's staff struck Robin's squarely and broke it cleanly in two at a fault in the wood. Robin jumped back quickly, raised his horn and blew three blasts.

"Blow all you will, outlaw," the tinker said. "I'll have you, awake or senseless, to take to Nottingham's Sheriff who'll pay me my 100 crowns."

The tinker raised his staff. Just then, Little John and his men burst from the woods. The tinker, thinking they were the Sheriff's foresters, called to them.

"You're just in time. I've captured Robin Hood, and I need your help to take him to Nottingham."

Little John aimed an arrow at the tinker. "That's our leader, and if you don't let him go, I'll leave a hole in you that even your tinker's skill can't mend."

"Nay, Little John," Robin Hood said. "This tinker has given me a good fight. Let us, instead, offer him a chance to practice his trade in our outlaw band."

"This time I've surely bitten off more than I can chew," the tinker said in amazement. "I see my golden crowns flying out the window."

"Fear not," Robin said. "We'll supply you with suits of green, plenty of tinker's work, good ale and food, and 50 gold crowns a year."

The tinker grinned. "How could I refuse such a generous offer...especially with yon giant still aiming his arrow at my gut. Your Sheriff can do his own dirty work."

Robin then clapped him on the shoulder, and all eight of them started for the Blue Boar Inn to quench their thirsts after so much excitement.

23

Robin·and·the·Tinker·
at·the·
BLUE·BOAR·INN·

Will Stutely Is Captured And Rescued

The Sheriff could find no one else to seek the reward for Robin's capture. The story of the tinker had travelled to all parts of the county. But when winter fled and spring's green leaves were bursting out, the Sheriff began to think. If he did not get Robin this year, the King might well replace him as Sheriff.

So he called all his men and said, "We will surround the forest with two men together every 500 paces. If anyone sees an outlaw, he shall blow his horn and all within hearing shall come running. Whoever captures Robin Hood will share 100 gold crowns. And there will be 25 gold crowns for each of his men."

No sooner had his men started for the forest, than one of Robin's men took the word to his leader. Many of the band wanted to fight the Sheriff's guards, but Robin decided they would hide for a week, reasoning that the Sheriff would soon give up.

Seven days later, Robin sent Will Stutely out to spy in a friar's costume over his Lincoln green. With his hood drawn up to hide his face, Will left the woods and walked to the Blue Boar Inn, for the owner and his family were good friends. There he found six of the Sheriff's men, drinking ale. Seeing them too late to turn around, he entered, sat with his face hidden and waited for the owner to come to his table.

But an inn cat, knowing Will in spite of his disguise, rubbed against his legs, pulling open the front of the robe. One of the guards was watching Will and saw the flash of Lincoln green. With a shout, he rushed Will and bashed him on the head with a heavy pewter ale mug. Will fell to the floor, unconscious.

Later, the daughter of the Blue Boar's owner ran panting into the outlaw camp. "Will was captured," she told Robin. "They say he'll be hanged tomorrow."

Robin thanked the girl, then shouted for his men to change into disguises before starting for Nottingham town.

The guards on the city's main gate had been doubled. Robin and his men hid at the edge of the woods and watched. The only thing moving outside the walls was an old palmer.

Robin called softly to David of Doncaster. "Wait until that pilgrim is away from the city wall, then meet him. He may know something about Will."

As the old pilgrim walked slowly along the road, David went out to meet him.

"Good day, father," David said politely. "I've been wondering whether to stop at Nottingham. Is anything interesting happening here?"

"Depends on what you'd call interesting," the old man grumbled. "They're going to hang an outlaw tomorrow at high noon at the crossroads."

"An outlaw?" David asked.

"That's what they call him, but from what I hear, he's just a poor fool who's tried to stay alive in this terrible time. I think it's a shame."

"Thank you, father. I guess I don't want to go to Nottingham today after all." The young man walked away.

The next morning, the Sheriff and his armed guard rode from the gates surrounding a cart. In it Will was tied erect, looking around defiantly. Behind the horsemen and cart ran scores of townspeople. As the procession moved away from the city, more and more people seemed to join the running throng.

Then Will saw a face he knew and realized all those around the cart were his fellow outlaws. Although the mounted guards yelled at them, they continued to cluster around Will.

Ahead at the crossroads, another group of spectators waited. Suddenly, those around the cart pulled it to a stop.

"What's this?" cried the Sheriff, reining his horse. "Let that cart go! Guards, scatter that mob!"

"I wouldn't do that, Sheriff," came a loud voice from the crossroads. The Sheriff whirled to see the ragged stranger who had won the archery contest. He was standing in front of 50 men with arrows aimed at the Sheriff.

"Back to the castle," the Sheriff shouted, and followed his own order by wheeling his horse and setting off at a dead run, bent low over the saddle. The guards followed his lead, and the scared townspeople who had been trailing the procession ran yelling after them.

Laughing, Robin and his men cut Will Stutely free and started back to the forest.

The. Aged. Palmer. gives. Yovng. David.
of. Doncaster. news. of. Will. Stvtely

CHAPTER 3

Little John Goes To The Blue Boar Inn

In Spring, Little John became restless. He had been cooped up for the winter and longed to get out and stretch his legs.

After defeating the Sheriff at the crossroads, Robin's band of merry men grew even larger as poor and hunted men came to them for haven. So many had come, often with women and children, Ralph of Wakefield and his helpers were running out of cloth to clothe them. That's when Robin decided that Little John should go to Lincoln to purchase more green cloth. Since the trip would take six days, Robin figured it would give Little John a chance to recover from the past winter.

He started out on Watling Street, but after a while Little John came to a crossroads. One way led to Ancaster and thence to Lincoln, while the other led off the highway to the Blue Boar Inn. Little John knew he must go on to Lincoln. But he was thirsty. Then he remembered he owed the owner of the inn a couple of pennies from last fall.

He decided to pay his debt in case anything should happen to him on the road.

The owner was glad to see him, and a number of fine fellows were sitting about since it was too early to work the fields. One thing led to another, and finally Little John decided to stay overnight at the inn.

Robin's scouts were now everywhere. That evening at dinner in the camp, someone mentioned Little John was spending the night at the Blue Boar.

"I'd better see to it John gets on his way, for there are several other inns he favors around here," Robin laughed.

Early the next morning, Robin left the camp alone, setting out for the inn. Little John also left early and was walking back to the main road when he saw a curious sight. There was a rustling in the leaves. A large head with a cap of thick cowhide appeared and disappeared every few moments. The head moved away and then disappeared completely into the woods. Curious, Little John followed the noises.

Little John Fights Arthur a Bland

Finally, in a little clearing, he saw the head again. It was attached to a thick, muscular body which was holding a bow and arrow ready to shoot at a deer.

"Hold!" roared Little John. The deer, startled, bounded out of sight. "What do you think you're

The·stout·bout·between·Little·Iohn·&·
Arthvr·a·Bland:·

doing?" Little John had come to think of the deer in Sherwood Forest as his own responsibility.

"Who wants to know?" the stranger asked.

"I'm a forester," Little John said, adding under his breath, "in a manner of speaking." "You were about to poach a King's deer!"

"But I didn't shoot." The man puffed up importantly. "Besides, do you know who I am?"

"Yes, a poacher."

"I'm Arthur a Bland, a tanner of renown."

"That explains it," Little John said. "You were looking for deer hide. Why, that's worse than killing to eat. Come with me, you...you... poacher!"

"Just try to take me, you big lummox," the tanner yelled, swinging his quarterstaff at Little John.

Little John raised his own staff, and the two went at it, striking and parrying, without either getting the upper hand. Neither of them saw Robin Hood slip up. He sat and waited for the giant to defeat the stranger.

Back and forth they fought. The staffs rose and fell, swung and thrust, warded and parried. Robin had never seen anyone hold out this long against his big lieutenant.

Then Little John swung his staff at the other man's head, but it bounced off the thick cowhide cap. Arthur a Bland just shook his head, then thrust his staff under Little John's guard and knocked the wind out of the giant. A hard blow to the ribs, and Little John was on the ground. The tanner raised his staff.

"Stop!" Little John yelled. "You wouldn't hit a man when he was down, would you?"

"Certainly," the tanner replied, waving his quarterstaff in the air, "particularly when it's a King's forester."

With that, Little John cried, "Hold, I give up." The tanner lowered his staff.

Robin Hood, laughing, stood up. "I never thought I'd see someone best Little John at quarterstaff. I'm Robin Hood."

The tanner stared. "I thought he was a King's forester. Had I known 'twas Little John, I never would have dared to oppose him."

"I'm glad you did," Robin said, looking at Little John, who was wincing as he got up. "He needed a comeuppance. How would you like to join our merry men?"

Arthur a Bland broke out in a great smile. "To be a member of your band? It would be a great honor — and lots of fun!"

Robin shook his hand, and Little John, more gingerly, did the same. Then Robin proposed they accompany Little John to see he didn't stray again from his path to Lincoln.

The Three Outlaws Meet A Fancy Gentleman

As the three friends walked along, they saw a traveler coming. Robin couldn't believe his eyes. He asked the others, "Have you ever seen such a pretty fellow? He seems ready for a party."

It was a young man, dressed all in red, with fancy lace at his wrists, long blond hair and a fancy peacock feather in his cap. He was holding a rose to his nose as he strolled.

Arthur a Bland was puzzled. "Something's wrong," he murmured. "There's more to this dandy than meets the eye. He moves too much like a fighter, and that sword seems well used."

But the other two paid no attention. Robin called, "Hold there, young sir. I would remove some of your worries from you."

"I have no worries," the youth said gently, still smelling the rose.

"Money is worry," Robin said, "and I would relieve you of it. Hand over your purse, sir."

The young man tossed away his rose, and his sword seemed to jump from its scabbard. "I have no purse, and wouldn't give it to you if I had," he said even more softly. "I've not bothered you. Let me pass."

"Put away that sword," Robin said. "It would fare ill against my quarterstaff. Get a staff from those trees along the road, and we'll dispute your money and passage."

The young man turned a cold eye on Robin, inspected his staff thoroughly, then nodded briefly. Instead of cutting a branch, he reached down and plucked a young oak sapling from the ground, roots and all. He used his sword to trim it into a staff.

Merry·Robin·stops·a·Stranger·
in·Scarlet :·

Arthur a Bland whispered, "I told you that youth wasn't what he seems."

Little John replied, "I think Robin is in for more than he bargained, tanner. The boy's not much like a dandy now." The two sat down to watch.

The lad in red finished his staff and swung at Robin, who countered the blow. Robin was swift and wily but managed to land only a few blows. The stranger in red was a good fighter and seemed to be stronger than Robin.

Then Robin landed a good blow to the other's arm, and the stranger retreated. Then rallying, he struck a flurry of blows, numbing Robin's arms and hands, and steadily forced Robin to the edge of the road. Robin glanced down to make sure of his footing, and the stranger struck Robin hard in the ribs. Robin hit the ground on his back.

Robin's friends jumped up, and the stranger turned to them with his staff at ready. "If you want a piece of this," he said, "decide whether you'll come at me one at a time or together." He was smiling slightly and didn't seem very worried.

"No," Robin said, rising stiffly. "Leave him alone. He's a mighty fighter, and it seems our fate to have come up against better men this day, Little John.

"You're not as silly as you look, young sir," Robin said. "What's your name?"

"I'm William Scarlock of Maxwell town. And you, sir?"

"Will Scarlock, you rascal," Robin roared. "I'm your uncle Robin, who taught you to shoot a bow on your twelfth birthday!"

The two fighters clapped each other on the back so vigorously that clouds of dust arose.

"Uncle Robin," his nephew said. "I was coming to find you, but I didn't expect you so far from Sherwood Forest."

"Why are you visiting me, Will? Did my sister Alice send you?"

"I had a little altercation with my father's bailiff. Somehow he broke his arm and six ribs," the boy said. "Mother did suggest I look you up."

"You young rascal, I bet there's a warrant out for you this very minute. But I can always use a strong young man in my band." Robin introduced the boy to Little John and the tanner.

Little John looked down at him and said, "You're too pretty for a Scarlock. To me, you'll always be Will Scarlet."

And that's how he was known from that time on.

The Four Outlaws Meet A Miller's Son

A few miles later, the four friends felt the pangs of hunger. Soon they saw a miller walking with a great sack of flour over his shoulder.

"Ho, miller," Robin sang out. "How would you like to share your flour with four famished men?"

"No, thank you," said the young man in flour whitened clothes. "I'm going to sell this sack of flour in Nottingham."

"No, tarry," Robin said. "Perhaps you might have a coin to spare." Robin believed in letting wealthy tradesmen share their wealth.

The young miller halted and looked carefully at the four, especially at tall Little John.

"All right," he sighed. "I have my money hidden in this flour." He swung the bag to the ground and thrust his hands into the contents. The four leaned over to watch.

Suddenly, he threw two great handsful of flour at them. With cries of pain, the four outlaws pawed their eyes. The young miller brushed off his hands and then began pummeling all four about the backs and shoulders with his quarterstaff. The outlaws tripped and fell, while the miller still beat them with gusto.

"Hold, hold, miller," Robin cried. "You've won, and I apologize. But stay your cudgel, I pray you."

"Will you go, then, and leave me to my own way?" asked the miller.

"As my name is Robin Hood, I pledge you no further harm." Robin laughed. "But it seems the harm has been to us."

"Robin Hood? Why, I was coming to Sherwood Forest to join your band."

"Why would you want to do that, youngster?" Little John asked, vigorously brushing flour out of his beard.

"Because my father died and the abbot of St. Mary's foreclosed on our mill. This bag of flour is the only thing I have left in the world."

"What's your name?" Will Scarlet asked.

The·Four·Yeomen·haue·Merry·
Sport·with·a·Stout·Miller·:·

"Much, the miller's son, and there's no better miller in all of Nottinghamshire," he said proudly.

"Good at beating sense into others, too, I see — or rather, feel," Robin said, touching himself all over to be sure nothing was broken. "Little John, this is twice we've lost today. Let's forget about Lincoln and return to the forest with these three new recruits."

He turned to Much. "As for you, we can always use a man who is clever, can use a cudgel so cunningly, and has a trade. Come, we'll talk about setting up our own mill in the forest."

And the five brave outlaws turned on their heels and walked arm in arm back to Sherwood Forest.

CHAPTER 4

Allan a Dale Tells His Story

t was obvious the newcomers needed training, so Robin called Will Stutely and told him to take Will Scarlet, Arthur a Bland, Much the miller's son and two other new men to find contributors to the treasury.

The six soon found there was little traffic on the highways — just local farmers who greeted the outlaws when they met. They knew Robin's band never bothered good common people of Nottinghamshire.

John Coxblood, one of the newcomers, told the news of Nottingham town, where he had lived. John had stolen a loaf of bread for his little daughter, who was starving because John could not find work.

"When my little Katy was sick this spring, a young minstrel came and sang for her — without pay," John marveled. "He sang so sweetly that crowds gathered outside my poor hut, just to hear him. I swear, from that day on, my little girl started to get better."

Just then, they were spotted by a group of the Sheriff's men on horseback, and the outlaws were forced to hide in a nearby swamp until the constables left. Discouraged, and with the sun setting, Will Stutely decided to go back.

As they entered the woods, Will Stutely's catlike hearing caught a sound. The six soon found a huddled figure beside a tiny brook. It was a boy in soiled minstrel's suit, and above him on a tree limb hung a harp.

John Coxblood said, "Why, it's the young minstrel who sang to my daughter. What's wrong with you, lad?"

"Go away, I want to die," came the muffled answer.

"Nonsense," Will Scarlet said. "Come with us, lad. Nothing's so bad it doesn't help to tell it to friends."

He and Much helped the minstrel up. Arthur a Bland took the harp, and all seven headed toward the outlaws' camp.

"What's this?" Robin Hood asked. "This is no rich guest to be entertained tonight."

While Will Stutely told Robin about the minstrel, that young man stared around with dazed eyes. "What's this place?" he asked. Then he said, "You're...you're Robin Hood, aren't you?"

"That's right, youngster," Robin said. "But what's happened? Will tells me you want to die."

The boy's face turned sad again. "There's no use living now," he said. Then his story poured out.

A wandering minstrel since he was 15, the boy had stayed one night at a castle, where he received coin for his songs and stories, the next night at a farmhouse, where he found only bed and food. But he was happy.

One day, he sang in the house of a wealthy freeman who had a lovely young daughter, just his age. They fell in love. He came back to the farmer's house again and again.

But the father had bigger plans for his daughter and told the minstrel to stay away. The minstrel obeyed but had just discovered the maiden's father was making her marry a wealthy neighboring

knight, a man older than her father.

"Now my heart is broken," the young man said. "My love won't disobey her father, but she will die if she's married to that old man."

"What's your name, minstrel?" Robin asked, "and how old are you?"

"Allan a Dale, sir," the boy replied, "and I've just turned 18."

Robin thought to himself 18 was his age when he became an outlaw. He resolved to help.

Little John said, "I know the father. It's Cluer Hill, and he's a close man with money."

"I have a plan," Robin said. "I'll need a ring, marriage banns to be published, and a priest to say the service. That will be a problem, for the high clergy don't like us, and the lower priests and friars are afraid, although they sympathize with us."

"Here's a ring," the Widow Jenkins said. Her oldest boy was now a full-fledged member of the band. "It served me well through 18 years of marriage."

"I'll write the banns," Clyde de Morrow said.

"And I, uncle, know where you might find a sympathetic friar to conduct the ceremony," Will Scarlet said.

Allan a Dale couldn't believe his ears. "But she's to be wed next week," he blurted out.

"Then," Robin said, standing up, "it's time we got busy!"

Robin Meets A Friar And Fights

Early the next morning, Robin Hood, with Will Scarlet, Little John and 50 men, started off for Fountains Dale, a hermit's retreat near Maxwell, where Will had been raised.

Will Scarlet told Robin about the friar they were seeking. "He's not an ordinary priest," Will said. "He's a big, fat man, of amazing strength, who was a soldier before he became a monk. He's the only friar I know who wears a sword and helm. He says God respects a strong servant."

"That sounds like the priest for me," Robin said.

"I'm not sure you'll be able to convince him to accompany you," Will said. "Many have tried to make him leave his hermit's cave, but the people all love him and keep him well supplied with food and ale."

Two days later, Will Scarlet told Robin they were near the friar's tiny shrine.

"I'll go on alone," Robin said. "So many armed men may not set well with him." He told his men to rest and walked into the woods.

Soon he heard a voice from the trees at the edge of a wide brook. There, eating a huge meat pie, a friar in short robes that barely came below his knee was talking to himself.

"Such a fine pie. Yes, a bountiful pie. There surely has been no pie like this before. It's a pie to delight the eye and the nose. It's a very paragon of a pie."

Robin coughed. The friar turned in surprise.

Robin said politely, "Good friar, I'm a poor stranger who has walked long this morning. Would you share your pie with me?"

"Begone!" the friar said unhospitably. "There's only just enough for one, and I am that one."

Robin, who was really hungry, became angry. "You'd deny a bit of food to a hungry man?"

"If it was my only food," the friar agreed, rising. He was a tall, fat man with a sword buckled about his waist. The friar clapped a steel helmet on his shaven head.

"Begone!" he repeated. "I have more need for this pie than you, for you don't look starving."

"You can say that, you fat pig?" Robin cried, pulling out his sword to teach the monk a lesson. He was met by the friar's sword. Slash and thrust and parry. The fight moved back and forth across the glen. With a sudden twist, Robin sent the monk's sword flying. The man spread his arms wide as if welcoming a sword thrust.

"No," Robin said. "You're a good swordsman. I would only have you carry me across that stream to the other side." Robin thought he'd humble the friar a bit.

Without a word, the friar gathered up his sword, let Robin climb onto his back and walked into the water.

"Here," Robin said. "you may also carry my sword, for it's clumsy."

The friar tucked it under his arm and waded

across the stream. Once across, Robin climbed down and found himself threatened by his own sword.

"All right, stranger," the friar said, "turnabout is fair play. You may carry me back."

He climbed up onto Robin's back, and a great burden he was. Robin said nothing however, and staggered across the stream. On the other side he collapsed, and the friar rolled off. As quick as lightning, Robin snatched his sword and held it against the friar's stomach.

"We must repeat this exercise," Robin said. The friar again let Robin climb on his back. But in the middle of the stream, the monk gave a mighty heave, and Robin landed in the water. The monk splashed on to the other side.

Robin rose angrily. As he climbed the bank, the friar struck Robin's sword from his hand.

"I think the tables are turned," the friar said.

"Maybe," Robin said, snatching up his horn and blowing three great blasts. Almost instantly Robin's 50 men appeared with bows and arrows ready.

The friar put two fingers to his mouth and whistled shrilly three times. A pack of 50 short tailed dogs ran from the trees and ferociously surrounded Robin's men.

"Hold, father," Will Scarlet called. "Remember me? I'm Will Scarlock, to whom you once told stories."

"Ah, little Will," the friar cried. "You're in bad company." But he called off his dogs.

Will Scarlet waded across and told the friar, whose name was Tuck, why they were there.

The friar glowered at Robin. "If you wished my help, why did you fight me?"

"I was hungry and became angry when you refused me some of your big pie," Robin said apologetically.

Friar Tuck smiled. "You couldn't know I'd been on a holy fast for five days. That pie was my first food," he said. Then he suddenly spun around, shouting, "My pie, where is my pie?" He was just in time to see his dogs finishing it.

Robin laughed. "We have food, though I was too anxious to stop and eat. Come join us."

Friar Tuck ate more than any four men. Finally, he said, "The food, if it's all that good, is a great temptation. I'll go with you."

Robin Spoils A Marriage But Rights A Wrong

The wedding day dawned clear and bright. Little John took a crew to the church and sent the porter home. They put garlands of June flowers on the altar, green boughs over the door for good luck, and every foot was swept and dusted by a dozen women from the outlaw camp.

Clyde de Morrow hung on the door the banns he'd written. Friar Tuck, in a new brown robe, quietly crept into a confessional to hide.

Soon a procession came in sight. Leading was the Bishop of York, surrounded by a dozen of his lesser clergy. He rode a great white horse and was dressed in fine robes, with precious stones stitched to the collar.

Beside him rode the abbot of St. Mary's, in fine linen. Then came the knight, Sir Stephen of Trent, tall and grey haired, who was dressed in fine velvet cloth with golden chains and rings.

Behind him came the maid Ellen, riding in a litter. Beside her rode her father, Cluer Hill. Finally came a dozen of the knight's men at arms.

The Bishop of York saw a gaily dressed figure standing before the church. It was Robin, disguised in minstrel's clothing. Ellen also saw him and her heart lifted. Then she saw it wasn't Allan, and it sank again.

"What are you doing here, minstrel?" the Bishop asked as his priests helped him from his horse.

"I've come to serenade the bride and groom, your Eminence," Robin said politely.

"Fine, fine," the Bishop said, entering the church. "We'll get right on with it, and you may serenade to your heart's content."

Everyone except the men at arms entered the church, the bride with tears running down her cheeks. Robin said in a loud voice, "What's this? The bride weeps and sighs. Can it be she's sad the groom is far older than her own father?"

The knight turned angrily, and the Bishop made clucking sounds. Robin merely said louder, "We must have a song to cheer her up."

Robin·Hood·steps·betwixt·
Sir·Stephen·and·his·Bride:

Allan a Dale ran up the aisle, knelt on one knee before Robin and took the harp. The bride dropped to her knees and embraced him tearfully.

The Bishop cried, "What is..."

The knight shouted, "Who is..."

The father exclaimed, "How did..."

And Robin roared, "Be quiet, all of you!"

Stunned, they looked at him. "This maid loves this boy, and I'm ashamed of you," Robin said.

He turned to the knight. "Sir Stephen, I'm sure you didn't know about her love for Allan a Dale, for you're an honorable man."

The knight drew himself up and said, "I can assure you, whoever you are, I did not know about this." He glared at the father. "I'll return her dowry tomorrow. Although I love the girl and would have taken good care of her, I will no longer stand here to be a laughing stock!" He spun and strode from the church.

Robin said quietly as he left, "I'm pleased to have met you, Sir Stephen. My name is Robin Hood."

The knight didn't hear, but the Bishop swiftly crossed himself. The abbot turned white, and the other clergymen huddled like sheep to be slaughtered. The bride's father looked at Robin in surprise.

Robin said, "I hope you give your blessing to your daughter and Allan a Dale."

The father responded quickly. "I wanted to make her a lady, but if she prefers this minstrel, I won't stand in the way."

Robin then asked the Bishop, "Will you perform this ceremony?"

The Bishop drew himself up and said, "Never!" He beckoned to his followers and stalked from the church.

"But the banns aren't posted and there's no priest," the bride's father complained.

"The banns are posted on the church door, and I'll cry them three times to all who are here," said Robin.

While Robin was proclaiming the banns, Friar Tuck stepped from the confession booth. "I'm a true Cistercian friar, ordained by the prior of Fountains Abbey himself. I shall perform the holy sacrament."

And so he did. When it was over, and the two were one, everyone kissed the blushing, smiling bride and shook Allan's hand. Then the father was sent home with an escort of Robin's men.

Robin, Ellen and Allan a Dale went back to Sherwood Forest where a great feast was prepared. Allan became a valued member of Robin's band of merry men. He and Ellen lived together there happily.

LITTLE·JOHN·journeys·in·holy·COMPANY:

CHAPTER 5

Two Friends Go Adventuring Outside The Forest

lear Weather was a time for adventure. Both Robin and Little John were anxious to get out and do something exciting.

"I think I'll go as a friar," said Little John. "I've noticed how well Friar Tuck lives, and I think I'll have some fine adventures as a pious clergyman." Friar Tuck made a face over a great piece of venison he was eating.

"I'll just stroll along the highway and see what will happen," Robin said. So the friends left by different trails.

Little John found his monk's robes very comfortable. However, he was so tall he really became a "curtail" friar, for the robe barely covered his knees. His faithful quarterstaff was not too different from a friar's walking staff.

On the highway, he soon overtook three young farm girls with baskets of eggs and cheese.

"Ho," Little John said merrily. "Where are you going? Today's not a market day."

The girls giggled, but one said, "We're taking this cheese and eggs to the Cock's Crow Inn."

"I'll help you." Little John took the three baskets. He strung two on his quarterstaff, which he held with his left hand. He carried the third basket in his right hand.

Laughing and singing, the three soon came to the inn. With a volley of giggles and goodbyes, the girls went around to the kitchen, while Little John stopped in front.

There he saw two black robed monks, one tall and thin, the other short and fat, just about to mount their plump, glossy horses. They sniffed at the plain, brown robed friar.

"This is too expensive for the likes of you," the tall one said.

"Belike you're right," Little John said cheerfully. He held the bridles of the horses as the monks mounted. Then he trotted between the horses out onto the highway.

"Let go!" cried the shorter monk.

"I wouldn't think of it," Little John said. "I'm going your way, so I thought we'd be good company for one another."

Paying no attention to their complaints, Little John trotted along briskly for several minutes. Then he pulled the horses to a stop.

"Perhaps I'm not going as far as you. So I'll ask you now to give a few pennies to a fellow priest." He looked at them expectantly.

"We have no money," the tall one said, nervously. Little John didn't look pious enough.

"It's terrible how those inns rob poor travelers like us," Little John said, sadly. "Don't you think we should pray for some money?"

He stared straight into the tall one's eyes. The monk reluctantly agreed, and both climbed down.

Little·Iohn·in·y̆·guise·of·a·Friar·stops·three·Lasses·

Little John knelt with them and loudly beseeched the Lord for money. The monks weakly added their "amens."

"Now look in your purses," Little John said. "See if our prayers have been answered."

Both monks reached into their purses and came out with empty hands.

Little John shook his head sadly. "That's strange. My prayers are always answered. Let's see if you might have missed something." He reached into each purse.

"Ah," he said joyfully as he pulled out coins. "You must have missed these in the lining. I knew

our prayers would be answered." The two monks watched him sourly. "Let's see, 20 gold crowns and five silver shillings in yours, and 10 crowns and 10 shillings in yours. I'll take only the third which my prayers brought and leave you each with the third from your prayers."

The two monks glumly climbed aboard their horses.

"Have a good ride," Little John yelled, swatting the horses, "and remember the power of prayer, brothers." Laughing, he turned and headed back to the inn for his quarterstaff and a cold ale before returning to the forest.

Robin Meets A Beggar And Changes His Appearance

Robin Hood took a different route and came out on the highway to Mansfield, where he saw a beggar sitting at the side of the road eating a big meat pie.

"Hey there, good fellow," the beggar said. "Join me for lunch. It's too much for one alone, and not enough to save 'till evening."

"Thank you," Robin said politely. "I have a piece of cheese to share with you." He took cheese from his purse.

"You're eating well," Robin said, looking at the ragged clothing the other wore.

"Aye, I've had good luck today," the beggar replied. "I found a farmhouse with the farmer away. His servant girl took a fancy to me. Eat hearty, tomorrow we may starve."

After they had dined, Robin asked, "Good beggar, would you join in a little joke? It may come out

handsomely for you."

"What have I to lose?" the beggar answered truthfully. "My clothing is all I own. What have you in mind?"

"I'd like to exchange clothes with you," Robin said.

The beggar looked wonderingly at Robin's fine green outfit. Half convinced Robin was crazy, the beggar exchanged clothes with him. The outlaw handed the beggar a gold coin.

"That's for being such a good fellow."

The beggar, resplendent in Lincoln green, clapped his heels in the air. "I'm a regular dandy now," he cried. He waved goodbye to Robin and skipped off down the road.

Robin smiled. "There's a good deed done, and I think I'll have good luck in these clothes."

Robin Invites A Corn Merchant To A Fine Dinner

Walking along whistling, Robin saw a horseman in the distance. As he came closer, Robin could see a very small man on a very large horse. He recognized a corn merchant — a merchant who bought all the corn at the fall harvest, telling everyone there was too much grain, and he could pay but a few pennies. Soon he had it all. Then all winter, he sold it for 50 times what he paid, saying, "There isn't any corn, so I must charge dearly." He was rich but hated.

As he saw Robin, the corn merchant's face wrinkled in disgust. He urged his horse to the other side of the road. But Robin darted over and caught the horse's bridle.

"Hold, kind sir," Robin said. "Please spare a penny for a poor man."

"Begone, beggar," the corn merchant snarled "All like you should be jailed for bothering honest men."

Robin tried not to laugh, for he would never call

Merry.
Robin
clad·as
a
Beggar·
stops·
the·
Corn·
Engr·
offer·
by·the·
Crofs·
nigh
Oller-
ton.

this merchant honest.

"Begone, I say," the merchant said again. "I must get to Nottingham before nightfall."

"Just one penny before you go."

"I've not one penny with me," the corn merchant said. "Even if Robin Hood himself were to search me, he'd find nothing."

Robin stood on tiptoe and whispered, "Look at me again. Have you ever seen a beggar with clean skin and hands? I'm no beggar."

The merchant looked suspiciously at Robin, who pulled out a purse and opened it to show the gleam of gold.

"See, I'm afraid of Robin Hood. I know he doesn't bother beggars, so I travel thus."

The merchant, convinced, looked more friendly. "But as a beggar you must walk," he said. "I, too, have protected myself, and I can ride comfortably."

"But I'm carrying 200 crowns," Robin said.

"Ha," the merchant said. "I, too, carry 200 crowns, although I'd never tell this to a soul. I can be searched all day, and it will never be found."

Robin widened his eyes in surprise. "I don't understand."

The merchant winked and whispered, "The secret is in my clogs."

Robin looked at the merchant's shoes with thick wooden soles. "I see nothing unusual," he said.

The corn merchant smiled thinly. "The money is cunningly hidden inside the soles. They must be pried apart to find my gold."

Robin shook his head in wonder. "I'd never have guessed. We're headed the same direction. If you're willing, I'll trot along beside you."

The merchant hesitated, then said, "All right, but you'll have to keep up with me." He started his horse walking toward Nottingham town.

Robin soon put his hand on the bridle and pulled the horse to a stop. "Wait a bit," he said to the surprised merchant. "I'd like to invite you to my home for dinner and entertainment."

"Where is your home?" the merchant asked. "I see not even a track around here."

"It's over there," Robin said, waving toward the nearby woods.

The merchant tried to pull free. "But that's Sherwood Forest," he said with a quaver in his voice. "There's nothing in there but Robin Hood." With dawning realization he looked at the beggar.

"I see you've heard of me," Robin said. "It's a humble place, but we've entertained fine gentry and clergy."

The merchant was shivering as if he had a fever. "No, no, you'll kill me," he cried. "Let me go, I pray you."

Robin was taken aback. "I wouldn't hurt a hair of your head. You'd have to pay for the entertainment, but I'd never harm you."

The merchant shook even more. "You might not hurt me, but there are those among your band who'll surely blame me for their own failures."

Then Robin understood. The merchant had cheated some members of his band and was afraid of what they would do. "I'll protect you, merchant."

"No, no," the man cried. He kicked his heavy shoes to the roadway. "Here, take my shoes, but let me go." With that, he jerked the reins so violently that Robin lost his grip, and the merchant galloped down the road.

"Never have I had a guest who insisted upon paying for not enjoying our food and entertainment," Robin mused, smiling after the disappearing corn merchant.

CHAPTER 6

A Sorrowful Knight Visits Robin And His Band

 ometime later, when Robin was hunting contributors, he was surprised to see a fully armored knight sitting on a horse in the middle of the highway.

The knight's head was bowed. When Robin, curious, walked up to him, the knight continued to stare sadly at his horse's mane.

"Sir knight," Robin said, "are you ill? Is there something I can do for you?"

The knight looked at the outlaw. "There's nothing anyone can do for me," he said.

"My father always used to say it helped to share one's troubles," Robin said.

The knight looked closely at Robin. "Thank you for the concern, good sir, but my plight is one of money. I would even borrow from the Sheriff of Nottingham, but he likes me not, for I'm not favored by his master, the wormy Prince John."

The Sheriff's name alerted Robin. "You're not a friend of the Sheriff's?" he asked.

"I'd rather call a diseased toad a friend — although, come to think of it, there's not much difference," the knight said, bitterly.

"You have no money?" Robin asked.

"No money, and I owe four hundred pounds to the abbot of St. Mary's. He's about to foreclose on my estate," the knight said.

"You must have spent overgenerously," Robin suggested.

"I spent everything to keep my son from prison," the knight said sorrowfully.

"What's your name, good knight?" Robin asked.

"Richard a Lea, and little honor that name now bears." He sighed.

"Come to my home," Robin said. "We'll sup, and telling me may help."

Listlessly the knight agreed, so Robin led him into the forest.

"Where are we going?" asked the knight, realizing they were in the woods. "Who are you, sir?"

Robin blew three blasts on his horn. "I'd like to be a friend, Sir Richard. My name is Robin Hood."

As the knight stared, a score or more men in Lincoln green stepped out of the woods with arrows ready.

"Put down your weapons, men," Robin cried. "This is Sir Richard a Lea, our honored guest. Hubert, run ahead and tell Simeon we'll have a feast in Sir Richard's honor."

Later, at dinner, Sir Richard told Robin his sad

Merry·Robin·stops·a·Sorrowful·Knight·

story. Sir Richard's son had entered a tournament, where he had opposed another young squire from Lancaster.

"They met head on, and both lances snapped into kindling," the knight told Robin. "But my son's luck was bad, and a splinter from his lance was forced through the other's helm and pierced an eye. My son's opponent was dead before he fell." The knight shook his head in dismay.

"But that was an accident," Friar Tuck said. "They can't blame your son!"

"I'm afraid they did," the knight said sadly. "The dead squire was related to the powerful Earl of Lancaster. They arrested my son. I paid a ransom of four hundred pounds, and then I was forced to pay another four hundred pounds to the other boy's family. I sold everything, including my wife's jewels, and was forced to borrow from the abbot of St. Mary's. I can't pay it back, and it's due tomorrow."

"What happens when you cannot pay, sir?" Friar Tuck asked.

"I lose my land, my castle, and everything else I still have," the knight said, shaking his head wearily.

"Can't we do something, Robin?" Will Stutely asked. "This was not Sir Richard's fault, yet it will beggar him."

Robin smiled. "We'll see what can be done." He asked the knight, "Where's your son now?"

"In the Holy Land, fighting the Saracens. We have to keep the infidels from regaining what we've won there," the knight said.

Robin turned to his lieutenants. "I think we should help this knight. We have the money. Let's give him the money he needs and some to see him through the winter."

The men cheered lustily. So it was done. Clyde de Morrow brought four hundred and fifty pounds, which was about all they had in minted money. Sir Richard was overcome with emotion.

When he found his voice, he said, "Robin Hood, I thank you and your men most sincerely, but I can't take money from you except as a loan." He was quite firm.

"Then we'll loan it to you for one year," Robin said.

Little John said, "I think our friend should be better dressed to see the abbot. Don't we have some velvet and other rich cloth, Clyde?" The clerk nodded.

Robin said, "This gift you can't refuse, sir knight. Three yards of each cloth so you and your wife can be properly dressed."

Will Scarlet said, "He should also have golden spurs for elegance."

Much, the miller's son, said, "And a gold neck chain so he looks a man of property."

"Thank you again," the knight said. "I've never spent such a pleasant dinner. But now I must go if I'm to pay my debt on time."

Little John said, "You lack a retinue of men at arms, sir."

Soon Little John had fifty men, each uniformed in a shirt of chain mail over Lincoln green, a steel helmet, a sword and a bow and arrows. Little John led the company.

"This is the finest retinue I've ever had," the knight said. "Your men are most military appearing."

"They are well trained, too," Robin replied. "Little John is our military chief, and I believe these men put even the King's to shame."

With the knight leading, the men at arms marched out of the forest.

Sir Richard A Lea Pays The Abbot

The abbot of St. Mary's was having a festive dinner party. The Sheriff of Nottingham, the abbot's lawyer, several monks and some of the Sheriff's men were dining richly.

"You believe Sir Richard won't be able to repay the debt?" the Sheriff asked.

The abbot said, "His estate has fallen into disre-pair and there's no evidence that he can raise the money."

Just then, at the abbey gate, the knight arrived. The watchman said, "I'll stable your horse and give him oats, sire."

"No," Sir Richard said, "we won't be here long enough for that." He strode into the main building.

Sir·Richard·pleadeth·before·the·Prior·of·Emmet·

As he stepped into the great dining room, all conversation stopped.

"Well, Sir Richard," the abbot said, "have you come to pay the money I loaned you?" He smirked.

"Can you give me more time in which to pay?" Sir Richard asked.

"Not a day," said the abbot, glancing at his lawyer. "The justicar has papers for you to sign."

"What kind of papers?" the knight asked.

"Papers giving me your estate in forfeit of the loan," the abbot said.

"But my estate is worth nearly double the debt," Sir Richard objected.

The Sheriff, carefully rehearsed, asked, "My dear abbot, what would you give him for a complete release of his property?"

The abbot pretended to think. "I'll give him one hundred pounds gold for his remaining interest."

The Sheriff turned to Sir Richard. "Is that agreeable, Sir Richard?"

"Never!" the knight said.

"You false knight," cried the abbot angrily, "you deserve nothing. I offered one hundred pounds out of the goodness of my heart."

"I'm no false knight," Sir Richard roared back. He turned and beckoned. "I only tested to see if you were a greedy moneychanger."

Little John came into the room and dumped bags of coin in the middle of the table.

"There's your filthy money, false man of God," the knight said, drawing his sword and slashing through the money bags. Golden coins rolled over the table and onto the floor. The abbot and the others fell backwards in their chairs, thinking Sir Richard was attacking them with his sword.

Sir Richard stormed out of the room with Little John at his heels. As the watchman watched in amazement, the knight and his armed men marched into the darkness.

The Bishop Of York Is Made A Guest

Nearly a year later, Robin and his band were watching Watling Street when they spotted mounted men riding south toward London. As the procession came closer, Robin was able to make out the rich cloak and fine horse of the Bishop of York. Behind the Bishop, Robin could see heavily laden pack horses. Robin and Little John stepped out into their way.

The Bishop halted. "Please stand clear, my good men," he said in a resonant voice. "I'm on my way to Canterbury. If you wish a blessing, it must be a brief one."

Robin smiled. "Have you forgotten us so soon, your Eminence? We met at the wedding of Sir Stephen of Trent and the beautiful Ellen Hill."

The Bishop crossed himself quickly. "Robin Hood, the outlaw," he said nervously.

"Yes, your Eminence. We've waited here to invite you to be our guest at dinner."

The Bishop looked quickly for an escape. Robin raised his horn and blew three times. Suddenly the woods erupted armed men.

"My men would enjoy your company," he continued. "Perhaps you would bless us in our endeavors." He grasped the Bishop's bridle.

The Bishop's face took on a thunderous expression, but he looked at all the outlaws and merely shook his head angrily as they entered the forest.

After a great feast and entertainment, Allan a Dale sang his sweet songs while everyone rested and listened.

Then, as night was about to fall, Robin stood. "We've enjoyed entertaining you and your followers," he said. "But all good things must end, and so it's time to speak of payment." He looked meaningfully at the Bishop.

"Nothing was said about payment when you brought us here," the Bishop said in surprise.

"True," Robin replied. "But we didn't expect such a large group or such big eaters. Frankly, our coffers are somewhat bare. Since your Eminence is so well known for his charity, perhaps you'd like to donate to a worthy cause."

The Bishop looked around nervously. "I have little with me, just a few supplies for the Archbishop of Canterbury."

"Little John," Robin called. "Please look through those packs and see if there's a little something the Bishop might wish to contribute to the cause of the needy."

50

Soon Little John had the packs off the seven horses. The contents were spread out on blankets.

"What would the Archbishop want with so much velvet and linen and felt?" Robin asked. "Little John, divide all that into three piles — one for the Archbishop, one for the poor and one as payment for this day's entertainment." The Bishop bit his tongue and said nothing.

Little John pointed to a wood chest bound in iron bands. "Here's something that's not cloth, Robin. Shall we open it?"

From the corner of his eye, Robin caught the Bishop wincing. "Certainly, Little John. Let's appreciate the gifts the Bishop brings his master."

To no one's surprise, the chest was full of gold coins. Little John called for Clyde de Morrow to count, while the Bishop watched in fearful fascination.

"Twelve hundred pounds," Clyde finally totaled. The Bishop shuddered.

"I believe we'll use the same measure," Robin said. "One-third for the poor, one-third for entertainment, and one-third for the Archbishop, who must be very wealthy if all his bishops bring such gifts." The Bishop turned red with anger.

"Your Eminence, we're all Godfearing men. I hope you'll conduct a mass for us before leaving."

Reluctantly, the Bishop stood. One of his priests brought surplice and other religious items, while Friar Tuck set up his portable altar. The Bishop glared at him, but said nothing.

Later, Friar Tuck remarked to Robin, "That was the fastest mass I've ever heard. I could hardly follow his Latin, it ran so rapidly from his tongue."

"Will the Archbishop believe him?" Will Scarlet asked. "I hear he's almost as greedy as our friendly Bishop." They all laughed.

Robin's Loan Returned With Interest

The day Sir Richard a Lea's loan was due, that gentleman started out early with his men at arms. He had used Robin's extra fifty pounds wisely, buying seed and supervising the planting carefully so his fields yielded a fine harvest. His castle had been refurbished, his animals well fed, and there was money in his coffers. He had a pack horse with the four hundred and fifty pounds Robin had loaned him, plus gifts for the band.

Late that afternoon, as the light was lowering, a worried Will Stutely said to Robin Hood, "I hope nothing has happened to Sir Richard. Otherwise he'd be here to repay his debt to you."

"Anything could happen," Robin said. "We'll not give him up for a day or two. He's a most honorable knight and will be here soon."

Just then, they heard the blast of a horn. Soon, into the big clearing came a mounted knight with fifty men at arms and pack horses. Leading them was a young man in torn clothing and bandages.

"Do my eyes deceive me," Will Scarlet said, "or is that our David of Doncaster who leads the way?"

The knight dismounted and clasped Robin's hand warmly. "I have come to..."

"Stop!" Robin interrupted Sir Richard. "No business before dinner. But where did you find this young rapscallion?" He looked searchingly at David, who blushed under the bandages.

Over dinner, Sir Richard told the story. He had gotten caught that morning in a crowd going to a fair in Wentbridge. He was carried along with them. At the fair, he was just in time to see David defeat the local champion wrestler.

David contributed that he had been coming back from visiting an uncle who was sick, when he was also caught in the crowd. Once at the fair, he'd been unable to resist the challenge of the local champion and had thrown him three times. Then the crowd got ugly.

"I barely reached him in time," Sir Richard said. "The crowd was trying to tear him apart. Only our arms prevented them from finishing him. I'm sorry to be late, but I thought you'd probably like David back, even a bit damaged." Everyone laughed.

With dinner over, the knight arose. "Friends, I've brought back your generous loan, together with a few gifts to show my wife's and my appreciation for your kindness."

His men opened the packs. The first held four hundred and fifty gold pounds. In the others were great long bows of yew wood, cunningly inlaid with silver, and one worked in gold. There were straight oak arrows with razor sharp steel points and fletched with peacock feathers.

"These are but poor tokens of our gratitude," Sir Richard said. "There's a silver bow for each of you, with a dozen arrows. For Robin Hood, a bow in gold. We hope each time you use these bows you'll remember our thanks." He sat down to a tumultuous cheering.

When everyone had admired their bows and arrows, Robin told the knight about dining the Bishop of York. "You see, he contributed twice the money we loaned you."

Robin turned serious. "Our treasury is overfull now, and I worry about its safety. Sir Richard, would you take the four hundred and fifty pounds which you brought here and invest it for us — in land, or animals, or in commerce? We must look to the future, and there's no one I trust more than you."

The knight said, smiling, "It would be an honor to assist you in such a small way. I'll put this money to good use for you, so it will multiply for the future."

That night there was great celebration, with much singing and dancing by the light of torches.

CHAPTER 7

Robin Becomes A Butcher And Meets Maid Marian Again

 aturally, a sunny spring day brought out adventure-some spirits. So one spring day, Robin and Little John were at breakfast.

"I've been cooped up too long," Robin said. "I need to stretch my legs."

"I feel the same way," Little John said, stretching. "It's time to go adventuring."

Robin and Little John decided to seek adventure separately, with each returning and telling their stories. Robin left for Nottingham, while Little John headed north to Worksop.

As Robin reached the highway, he saw a butcher coming in a cart. Robin hailed the man. "What goes on about here?" Robin asked.

"It's market day in Nottingham," the butcher answered, "and I hear Prince John is in town."

"Would you like to sell all your meat at once?" Robin asked.

"Indeed," the butcher replied, "but I have at least four crowns worth in my cart."

"How much for the cart and horse?" Robin asked.

"At least four crowns more," the butcher said.

"Done," Robin cried. He pulled out his purse and counted out eight gold crowns into the amazed butcher's hand. He bought the man's apron and knife for another four shillings. The butcher left, eager to tell his family about his wonderful luck.

Robin, laughing to himself, put on the apron, hid his bow and quarterstaff in the cart, and drove to Nottingham.

He found the streets already crowded, and he had to hunt for a space in the square to set up his table. The other butchers were crying, "A penny a pound, a penny a pound for the finest flesh," over and over.

Robin's cry was different. "Three pounds for a penny, for meat that is sweet," he called.

Soon there was a line at his table. Housewives jostled cooks from wealthy houses. The other stands were deserted.

Some of the other butchers gathered to watch Robin. "That boy's crazy," an older butcher said.

"No," a younger one said, "he doesn't look like a butcher. I'll bet his father's died and left him the business."

"I think you're right," another said. "He doesn't even know how to cut meat properly."

The older man shrugged. "He'll be sold out in another half hour. Then we can get about our own business."

Robin was having a fine time. If he cut too much, he gave the buyer a wink and a smile. If he cut too little, he threw on another piece.

The Sheriff's wife was concerned that Prince John would be dining at the castle when he and the Sheriff came back from hunting. "Come, Marian," she said to the girl who was visiting her. "We'll go to market with the cook."

When the three reached the square, they saw all

Robin·turns·butcher·and·
sells·his·meat·in·Nottingham:

the crowd around one table. "What can that be?" the Sheriff's wife asked.

The cook, who'd heard Robin's call, started to run. "It's a sale of meat," he shouted over his shoulder. The women followed more slowly.

"That butcher with the yellow beard," the Sheriff's wife said thoughtfully, "doesn't he seem familiar to you?"

"One butcher looks like another," the maid Marian said casually. But she recognized Robin. In the two years since the archery match, she had often thought of him.

Robin felt someone looking at him and glanced up as he cut. There, at the edge of the crowd, was the girl he had kissed at the shooting match. He winked at her. She smiled and blushed.

When the castle cook reached the table, the meat was almost gone. The cook pulled out his purse and said, "I'll take it all, butcher."

"If you're with these lovely ladies, you may take it for nothing," Robin said, laughing. "I'll collect from the ladies. Will you pay a kiss for the meat?" he asked.

The Sheriff's wife drew herself up in disdain. But Marian stepped forward, leaned over the table and gave him a long kiss. Robin grinned widely, Marian blushed again, and the crowd cheered good naturedly. The Sheriff's wife grabbed Marian's arm.

"I don't know what's come over you," she hissed. "Kissing a strange man!" She pulled Marian back to the castle.

The crowd was drifting to the other tables, but the younger butcher came to Robin and said, "You're new here, so you may not know we always have supper at the castle. Prince John himself will be there tonight."

"I'll be there, too," Robin said. He smiled to himself. The Sheriff would be entertaining Robin Hood.

Robin Enjoys The Meal And The Company

That night, Robin was led into a great dining hall where most of the butchers were already seated. At the head of the table sat the Sheriff, with his wife on one side and the unpleasant looking Prince John on the other. Maid Marian sat next to the Prince.

The young butcher stood and beckoned to Robin. "Come, I've saved a place for you," pointing to a place across from maid Marian.

"Thank you," Robin said. Before sitting, he bowed to the Sheriff and the Prince. The Sheriff nodded his head; Prince John stared haughtily. Marian smiled a welcome.

The Sheriff was curious about this young man he'd heard had inherited a butcher's business. "Young man," the Sheriff said. "This is your first year here, and I hope we see you again in other years."

"Thank you, sire," Robin said, "but I may not stay a butcher. The pay is only occasionally good." He smiled at Marian, who blushed.

"What will you do with your business, then?" the Sheriff asked.

"I'll probably sell it," Robin said.

The Sheriff, smelling a profit, asked, "Do you have any horned beasts?" He was thinking of cattle.

"I have a large herd," Robin said, thinking of all the deer in the forest.

"How many do you have?" Prince John asked.

"About two hundred, your highness," Robin answered. "I've never counted them."

The Sheriff and the Prince smiled at each other. They put their heads together as Robin ate and looked at Marian.

Finally, the Sheriff said, "Young man, I'd be interested in buying your herd. What would you ask?"

Robin thought. "Probably two crowns a head."

The Sheriff, knowing he could get at least four crowns each for cows, plus two crowns for the hide, cried, "Done! I would see your herd. Is it far?"

"Not far," Robin said. "We could reach there tomorrow if we left early." So they agreed to leave at seven the next morning.

Robin, at the end of the meal, said, "I've enjoyed this meal greatly, and the company even more. A toast to good health and successful business."

Everyone smiled and drank. The Sheriff invited Robin to stay at the castle for the night.

Robin was shown to a room in one of the castle towers. When he was getting into bed, he heard a rap at the door. Opening it, sword in hand, he was surprised to see maid Marian slip in.

"Robin Hood..." she whispered, then stopped because he was kissing her. Then, although her heart was beating rapidly, she pulled away and said, "I heard the Sheriff and Prince John talking. The Sheriff's going to buy your herd, then take most of the money back as taxes. You must get away before they find out you're Robin Hood."

He reassured her. They sat for almost the whole night, holding hands and telling each other about themselves. Just before dawn, the maid Marian slipped back to her room, but not until she and Robin had promised to meet again.

At six, Robin had breakfast with the Sheriff. Soon, with a dozen of the Sheriff's men, they rode along the highway north.

"We leave the road here," Robin said, pointing to a trail into Sherwood Forest.

"But that's where Robin Hood and his outlaws lurk." The Sheriff stopped his horse.

"It's the shortest way to my herd," Robin said. "I can lead you safely through."

Reluctantly the Sheriff followed. In a short time they came upon a large herd of deer. Robin raised his horn and blew three loud blasts. The deer ran.

"Why did you frighten the deer?" the Sheriff asked.

"I wanted you to see them run," Robin replied. "Isn't my herd of horned beasts a fine one?" He laughed.

The Sheriff quickly understood. "Grab him, men! He's an outlaw!"

"Robin Hood, at your service, sire," Robin said, backing his horse away.

Just then, two score men in Lincoln green appeared with arrows pointed at the Sheriff and his men. "Meet my merry men," Robin said. "Come and have dinner with us. We haven't had such an important guest since the Bishop of York."

Little John Fights And Is Hired

When Little John left Robin, he decided to look over a country fair at Worksop. Three hours later, he arrived to find the town full of farmers and a hunting party of nobles. They were watching two men fighting with quarterstaves. One of the men was soon tumbled to the ground, defeated.

An official in the ring shouted over the crowd's cheering, "Eric of Lincoln has won another round. Is there anyone who will risk a match for a gold crown to the winner?"

Little John raised his staff. "There's a likely looking fellow," the official cried. "Let him through."

When Little John reached the platform, he realized Eric was a man about his own height, which was very unusual. They shook hands. "Let the fight begin," the official shouted.

The men were evenly matched. Little John was heavier, but Eric was quicker. The match moved back and forth with both men giving and taking hard blows. Little John remembered how he had beaten Robin Hood on the log. He stepped back as if to catch his balance, then thrust his staff into the other's unprotected stomach. As Eric doubled up, Little John hit his head. The champion fell to the floor.

The crowd went wild. A fat noble on horseback beckoned to Little John. After getting his gold coin, Little John waded through the crowd to the horseman, whom he recognized as the Sheriff of Nottingham.

"I must have him for my guard, Prince John," the Sheriff was saying to the man beside him.

"Tell me, fellow, would you like a good job for five pounds a year?" the Sheriff asked Little John.

Little John thought it might be fun. "Certainly, sire."

"What's your name?" the Sheriff asked.

Little John thought quickly. "Reynold Greenleaf," he said, using an old family name.

"Fine. Mount behind one of my men, Reynold." The Sheriff and Prince John turned their horses and started away.

Little·John·overcomes·Eric·o'·Lincoln

Little John Fights For His Breakfast

At Nottingham Castle, "Reynold" had dinner with the other guards. Afterward, they gambled and talked in their quarters until late. Little John awoke late in a room he didn't recognize. Then he remembered where he was. Hungry, he looked for the kitchen.

"Here now," the castle steward said when he found Little John outside the pantry. "Breakfast is over!"

"But I'm hungry," Little John said reasonably.

"Doesn't matter, you'll have to wait for lunch," the steward snarled. Not in a good mood anyway, Little John shoved the steward against the wall. The man's head hit the plaster and he slid unconscious to the floor.

"I hardly touched him," Little John mused. "Must have a soft head." He went into the pantry and started to eat a meat pie.

A big, husky cook came in, looked and rushed out again. Little John ate on.

"Get out of here, you big lummox," a voice said angrily. Little John looked up to see the cook holding a sword. Quickly he jumped up and unsheathed his own weapon.

Swinging lustily, Little John backed the cook out into the kitchen, where the kitchen help ran squealing away. Back and forth they fought, for the cook was an excellent swordsman. Finally, Little John caught the other's blade, and it flew out of the cook's hand.

"I give up!" the cook cried.

"I just want to finish my breakfast in peace," Little John said. "Join me?"

The cook realizing he, too, was hungry after the swordplay, helped Little John finish off the meat pie and several mugs of ale.

"You're a fine swordsman," Little John remarked. "Why are you a cook?"

"I was once a man-at-arms like you," the cook replied, "but I was wounded in battle, and they put me to work in a kitchen. I found I like cooking."

Little John found out the cook, whose name was Alfred, hated the Sheriff. "How would you like a job as a cook for five score men, with lots of women and children to help in the kitchen?" Little John asked, knowing Simeon was tired of the job.

The cook said, "It sounds like Robin Hood's band."

"You're right," Little John said. "You'd get 50 golden crowns a year, and a chance to use that sword now and then."

The cook poured two more mugs of ale. "I've had enough here," he said, raising his mug. "I'll go with you."

The two new friends decided they should take some souvenirs. As a member of the Sheriff's guard, Little John got two horses from the castle stables, and the two men rode away with bags of the Sheriff's silverware behind their saddles.

At the camp, Robin kept the nervous Sheriff and his men occupied all afternoon watching shooting at targets, jousting and wrestling. Just as dinner was ready, Robin heard a sentry call, and two large men rode into camp.

Robin warmly greeted Little John and his new recruit. The Sheriff's face turned red in anger as he recognized his cook and "Reynold Greenleaf," but he said nothing.

At dinner, Robin watched the fat man discover the silverware and plates were his. Still he said nothing.

When they finished, Robin rose. "Sheriff, we've enjoyed entertaining you. It's now time to guide you back, but it's our custom for our guests to donate to our charity fund. I think the 200 crowns to buy my herd would be just right."

The Sheriff winced but untied his purse. "Between that and my finest silver, you've taken a lot from me this day," he growled.

"Nay, Sheriff," Robin said. "Your silver will go back with you. It's much too fine for a forest feast. Little John and our new recruit merely brought it to entertain you properly."

The Sheriff, with his silver service, rode back to Nottingham, where Prince John waited, wondering what had happened to their scheme to buy a cattle herd at far less than its value.

The·Mighty·Fight·betwixt:
Little John· and·the·Cook:

CHAPTER 8

Good Queen Eleanor Sends For Robin Hood

here was momentous news after several months. King Henry died. His eldest son, Richard, ''The Lion Hearted,'' was King. Everyone rejoiced.

One day, a sentry found a young page in the forest. The sentry brought him to Robin.

"I'm Richard Partington, page to Queen Eleanor," the richly clad youth said. "She's now in Leicester and is granting amnesty to all persecuted men."

"She's been released from Winchester?" Will Scarlet asked.

"Yes, since Richard became King. This past month she has traveled through much of England freeing prisoners, but she grows weary and asks you come to her to receive her pardon. I must ride on to Lincoln and York, bearing her messages to sheriffs there." He smiled. "Your own Sheriff of Nottingham didn't seem pleased the Queen is granting amnesty to victims of the Forest Laws."

"I shall go at once," Robin said. "But rest a bit before you ride."

The page agreed to eat and rest. Robin spoke to Little John, Will Scarlet and Allan a Dale. "You three will go with me. Dress inconspicuously and be back here in an hour."

Young Partington, rested and fed, left to the north. Robin and his three men left for Leicester, a two-day walk to the south.

When they arrived in Leicester, they were directed to the castle. A uniformed guard took their names and disappeared. Soon he was back with a page, who guided them into the great hall. There the Queen sat on a throne, surrounded by many people.

"Robin Hood and his men," bawled the youthful page at the top of his lungs. Heads turned toward the four.

"Come closer," the Queen said in the silence. The four walked forward and knelt. "Rise," the Queen said, smiling.

"I've heard much about your exploits, Robin Hood, especially from this young lady." She nodded at a girl nearby.

Robin realized it was the maid Marian, smiling at him. But as he smiled back, he saw Prince John and the Bishop of York with their heads together.

"You seem to have many friends," the Queen continued. "A valiant knight told me of your heritage, Robert Fitzooth." She turned, and Robin saw she was looking at Sir Richard a Lea, who smiled at him.

"I wished to see such a legend — who robs the rich and gives to the poor — with my own eyes. I wished to give you and your men amnesty with my own hand." An official handed her two scrolls of parchment.

ALLAN·A·DALE·SINGETH·BE-
FORE·OVR·GOOD·QVEEN·EL=
EANOR·

·MDCCCXXCIII·

"From this day forward, you are absolved of all blame for past deeds," she said.

Robin stepped forward and took the scrolls. "Your majesty," he said, "you and King Richard have no more faithful servants than my men and I."

The queen placed her hand upon Robin's arm. "Promise to give up outlawry and leave the forest. I'm leaving England for Aquitane, and I want to know you'll take up a life of peace."

Robin bowed deeply. "You have my pledge, your majesty," he said. "We'll find honest work and be good subjects."

The Queen smiled again, and he and his men backed from the throne. Two people were waiting for them outside the hall, Sir Richard and the maid Marian.

"Robin, I'm so glad you're no longer an outlaw," Marian said. "Perhaps now I'll be able to see you."

"I, too, am pleased," Sir Richard said, clasping their hands. "When I return to Nottinghamshire, we'll speak about what you and your men can do now."

A page came from the hall and said the Queen would like to have all six of them join her for an informal supper in her chambers. The page of-fered to guide Robin and his men to rooms where they could freshen up. Robin and Marian parted reluctantly.

At the meal, the Queen told of her 15 years of captivity by King Henry and talked enthusiastically about King Richard and his plans. Afterward, the Queen said, "Allan a Dale, I hear you're a fine minstrel. Would you sing for us this night?"

Allan replied he had no harp. A page hurried out and returned a few minutes later with one Allan tuned. He sang while the Queen relaxed. Robin and Marian held hands and smiled at one another. Allan sang of love and adventure and pain and tears, and everyone could feel them in their hearts.

Finally, the Queen thanked him and dismissed them all, for she was leaving early the next day.

"I must leave, too, for my home in Sheffield," Marian told Robin regretfully, "but I hope I'll see you again soon, now you can travel without fear."

"I'll accompany her majesty to London," Sir Richard said, "but I should be in Nottinghamshire within the month."

Robin and his men were shown to rooms where they stayed the night.

Prince John And The Bishop Of York Chase Robin

Early the next morning the four friends started back to Sherwood Forest. By the time they had walked six hours, they were hungry and thirsty.

"Is that an inn ahead?" Will asked Little John. "You're so tall you should be able to see it better."

The inn was a small one, but had good food. Just as they were finishing lunch, they heard a horse gallop up outside. A man in the livery of Sir Richard entered. "Are you Robin Hood?" he asked.

"Yes, does Sir Richard seek me?" Robin replied.

"He sent me to warn you. The Bishop of York and Prince John have decided to murder you before you can return to Sherwood Forest. Sir Richard got word of it before he left for London."

The four friends were angry but not surprised. "What are we going to do?" Allan a Dale asked Robin.

"We separate right here," Robin said. "Each takes a different route. It's only ten hours to Sherwood. We each have a better chance alone." He turned to the messenger. "Thank Sir Richard for the warning."

"There's more. King Richard has promised the Pope to lead a third crusade to the Holy Land and will only be in England a few weeks before leaving for Palestine," the messenger said. "With both Richard and the Queen away, Prince John will be unchecked."

The messenger shook hands and left. The four friends wished each other luck and started out. Robin took a roundabout route. By following country trails, he made slower time, but had less chance of being sighted by Prince John's soldiers. When he arrived at Grantham, there didn't seem to be any soldiers about, so he boldly walked into town.

He stopped to talk to the guard at the gate. "I

Stout · Robin · hath · a · narrow · escape ·

hear Prince John's men are thick about here."

The guard shook his head. "Not that I know of. They haven't come by this gate."

Robin hurried through the town. On the other side, he left the main highway and took a farmer's trail. Tired, he started looking for a place to stay the night.

The next morning, Little John was the first to arrive at Sherwood Forest. About noon, Will Scarlet walked in. That afternoon, Allan a Dale wearily made his way to the glade. By sundown, all were worried about Robin.

"Don't worry," Will Stutely said. "Robin can take care of himself."

"He's the match for five or six of Prince John's men," Friar Tuck added.

But Robin was having problems. That morning he left the haystack where he slept and came to a stream, where he knelt to drink and wash his face.

Suddenly an arrow whistled past his ear.

Robin dived into the brush. He ran crouched behind a fence for several yards, then into a dense thicket. He could hear the excited calls of men behind him.

Regaining his breath, he worked his way deeper into the woods. He didn't know one of the Prince's detachments had stopped at each church along the route, asking for a man of his description. One of the Bishop of York's priests in Grantham remembered seeing him on the street.

The woods ended just below the top of a small hill. Robin could hear the Prince's men still beating through the brush behind him. Too late, he saw six men wearing the livery of the Sheriff of Nottingham on horseback on the road below. Turning, Robin ran back into the woods. A cry from below told him the Sheriff's men had sighted him. Now there were two groups hunting him.

Robin Hides In A Hole And Stays Whole

Then Robin tripped and fell to the ground. About to bound up again, he saw that he'd caught his foot on a tree root. The soil had washed out from under it, and there was a small cave formed by the hollow under the root.

Quickly he cut a small bush growing nearby. Rolling into the hole, he arranged the bush outside to hide the opening. Then he settled himself to wait.

He could hear the soldiers and constables getting closer. Then he heard the thud of horse hooves right beside his ear. A constable was sitting on his horse, not five feet from Robin's hiding place. Robin could see him clearly from his hole behind the bush. The constable looked around, then went on.

The sounds died away, but Robin stayed quiet. Finally, he fell asleep. It was night when he awoke. "Fine," he thought, "I'll get back to Sherwood safely in the dark."

About midnight, a sentry in the forest was startled to hear a voice whisper in his ear, "I'm glad to see you awake at your post, Arthur a Bland." It was Robin, home again.

It was fortunate Robin's band had everything they needed in the forest, for the Prince and the Sheriff put guards around it. Not even a hare could

have sneaked out. At night torches ringed the woods. Robin was puzzled, for keeping so many men there was costing their enemies a great deal of money.

Then, three months after it started, a sentry reported the entire force had left. Robin sent one of the newer men into Nottingham town.

"King Richard has been in England and has left again for the Holy Land," the man reported. "Queen Eleanor is still in France."

"That's it," Robin told his lieutenants. "Prince John kept us here until King Richard left England. He made sure we couldn't tell the King about Prince John's treachery."

"But what shall we do now, Robin?" Friar Tuck asked.

"Until the Queen returns, or until King Richard gets back," Robin said, "we'll have to hide here in Sherwood. However, instead of robbing all the wealthy, we're going to limit our attention to the Sheriff, Prince John and the Bishop of York, and their men. When King Richard or Queen Eleanor come back, we'll be able to prove we're no longer outlaws, but are just protecting ourselves and others against those false men who make mockery of the Queen's mercy."

ROBIN·and·LITTLE·JOHN· go· their· ways· in· search· of· Adventure:

CHAPTER 9

Robin Fights Guy Of Gisbourne In The Forest

All Nottinghamshire marveled at the change in Robin Hood's band. Rich merchants, fat priests, important nobles, all could travel the highways of Nottinghamshire safely. The county might have gotten a reputation of most law-abiding in all England, but there were three exceptions. Prince John's men who came into the area were ambushed and stripped of everything. Each one was left with only a sheet to wrap himself in. Soon, Prince John, who was busy intriguing in London, stopped sending men into Nottinghamshire.

The same fate met the Bishop of York's priests and friars on their way to London and Canterbury. Finally, all such trips were routed far around the county, taking an extra five or six days' travel.

The Sheriff's men were so harassed they would not even leave the gates of the town unless there were fifty or more of them at a time. The collection of taxes slowed down.

The Sheriff couldn't let it continue. Without taxes coming in, his own income was drying up. He sent a messenger to the Bishop of York. The Bishop made a deal with a vicious outlaw in his county. Guy of Gisbourne left for Sherwood Forest to kill Robin for the Sheriff.

One morning, walking in the forest, Robin felt someone nearby. There was a clearing nearby, so he kept to cover as he approached it.

He saw a most curious sight. A man as big as Robin himself was standing there, covered in horsehide. Even the head of the horse was stretched over the man's steel cap. And this strange looking person was heavily armed with sword, bow and quarterstaff.

Robin backed off, then whistling, walked along the trail through the glade. When he saw the stranger, Robin acted surprised. "Ho, there. I didn't think I'd meet anyone here, since everyone's so afraid of Robin Hood."

"That's who I hope to meet," the stranger said.

"You have business with Robin Hood?" Robin asked, looking amazed. He stepped back. "You're not an outlaw, too?"

"Yes, but my business is only with Robin Hood. I've been paid to kill him by the Sheriff of Nottingham."

"But Robin Hood has many men," Robin said. "How will you do it?"

"I'm Guy of Gisbourne," the other boasted. "I kill from ambush. I've killed 20 men that way.

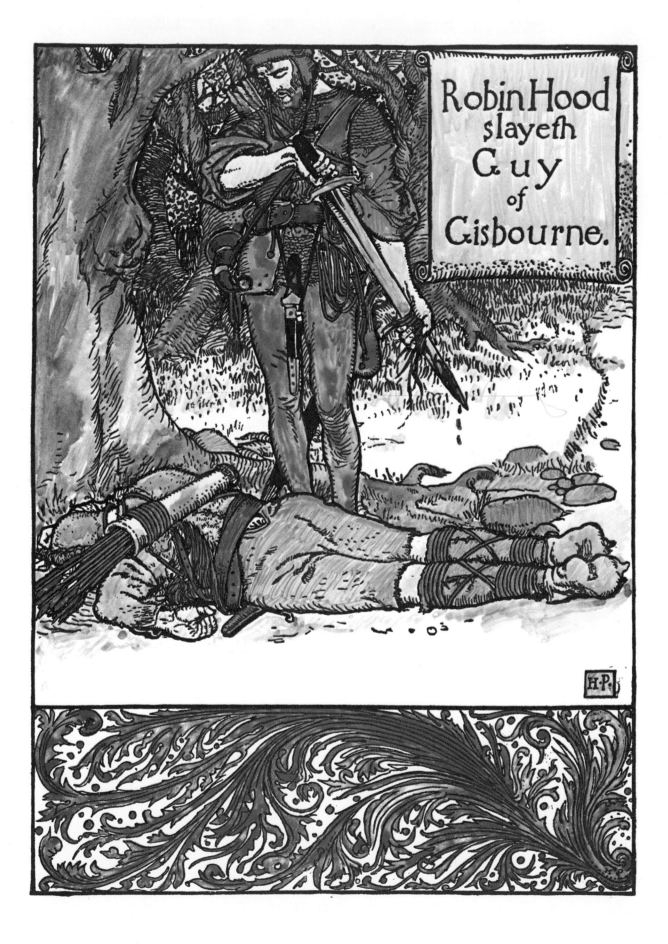

Robin Hood
slayeth
Guy
of
Gisbourne.

Where can I find Robin Hood?"

"About 10 feet in front of you," Robin said grimly, pulling his sword.

With a shout of surprise, Guy pulled his own sword. They were well matched, but Robin slashed and thrust and kept the other moving backward. More than once, Robin's sword struck the other, but the tough horsehide turned aside the blade. Robin was bleeding from several small cuts made by Guy of Gisbourne's sword. Both began to tire.

Robin decided to use one of his father's tricks. He stumbled and fell to one knee, with his sword point on the ground. The other gave a wild cry of triumph and swung his sword for a slash at Robin's head.

Robin whipped his sword point up to slash the other's unprotected legs. Attempting to jump back, Guy of Gisbourne fell forward instead and was impaled upon Robin's raised sword. He fell dead beside Robin.

Robin got up and pulled his sword from the dead man. "I've killed a man," Robin thought. "I didn't intend it, but I'm not sorry such a terrible man is dead."

Seeing a curious horn beside the body, Robin lifted it to his mouth and blew a strange, mournful note. Within a few minutes, Robin heard a large body of men coming.

He pulled Guy of Gisbourne behind a tree, stripped off the man's strange horsehide armor, and put it on with the horsehead hiding his face.

The Sheriff led a troup of armed men. "Well, Gisbourne, I hope you've killed Robin Hood as we agreed."

Robin answered in a gruff voice. "The outlaw's dead, sire, but he had a most curious horn." He lifted Robin's silver horn and blew three times.

"What in blazes did you do that for?" the Sheriff yelled. "That's how the outlaws signal."

"If you leave now, you can probably get away safely," Robin said. He pulled back the horsehead.

"Cut him down, men!" the Sheriff cried. But before his startled guards could act, more than 50 of Robin's men appeared.

The Sheriff wheeled and raced away, lying flat along his horse's back. Little John couldn't resist. He let fly an arrow. The Sheriff screamed as he disappeared through the trees with an arrow in his fat rump.

Sir Richard Seeks Money For King Richard's Ransom

The Sheriff hid in Nottingham, and the attempts to capture Robin and collect taxes stopped. Robin knew something was wrong.

Then a sentry brought Sir Richard a Lea to the camp. He was tired and dusty from traveling. "I've come directly from London," he said.

He dismounted, and his knees buckled. Friar Tuck put out a mighty arm to support him.

"I've ridden without stop," Sir Richard gasped. "King Richard's a prisoner of Count Leopold of Austria. Prince John has kept it hidden."

There was an angry murmur from the men. Will Scarlet said, "I thought His Majesty was in the Holy Land."

"He was on his way home overland when he was captured and held for ransom. Prince John imprisoned the messengers. He hopes his brother will be killed so he can be King."

"How can we help?" Robin asked.

"Those faithful to King Richard are raising the money for his ransom," Sir Richard said. "But no money comes from Nottingham or York, where the Sheriff and Bishop support Prince John. Can you help?"

"How much is needed?" the band's treasurer, Clyde de Morrow, asked.

"Ten thousand pounds, and all is raised except 800 pounds," Sir Richard said.

"How much is Nottingham's share?" Clyde asked.

"Five hundred pounds," the knight answered. "A full year's tax collection from the county."

Clyde turned to Robin in amazement. "That's less than half of what the Sheriff collects. He's been taking half the tax money for himself."

At this, a roar of rage arose. Robin waved for silence. "Sir Richard, there should be more than that in the castle vaults. Rest and eat, while Little John and I plan a strategy."

The next Sunday, one of the Bishop of York's priests was holding services in Nottingham cathedral. He faltered in the Mass when Robin sat in the front row. He whispered to an altar boy, who scurried out of the church. Robin smiled to himself and quietly left.

When the Sheriff received the message, he rubbed his hands together gleefully. "Captain, take your guard out and surround the cathedral." The captain of guards rushed out, calling his men.

As soon as the guard left, two of Robin's men called to the one remaining guard on the gate. When he looked out, they grabbed, tied and gagged him and stuffed him back into the sentry box. Then they let in the rest of the men and four pack horses. The gates were locked behind them.

Robin and Little John found the Sheriff still at breakfast. His eyes rolled in fright as the two men pointed swords at him.

"We're in a hurry, sire," Robin said, mockingly. "Let's have the key to the vaults!"

"But that's robbery…" the Sheriff started to say. Instead, he unfastened the big key from his belt. "You'll never get a chance to spend any of it."

"It's not for us, Sheriff," Robin said. "It's your contribution to King Richard's ransom. Prince John will be pleased to hear how you came to his brother's aid."

The Sheriff turned white and started shaking at the thought.

Little John, cautiously approaching the cellar vaults, waved for a silent advance. Robin saw two great ironbound doors with an elderly armed guard sitting in front of them. Robin and Little John stepped into sight.

The man jumped up. "It's about time," he said sharply. "I certainly hope you brought the key." He held his hand out.

Robin and Little John looked at each other in amazement. Robin said, "We're not the Sheriff's men…"

"I know, I know," the man interrupted, "you're outlaws. Probably Robin Hood himself. And you must be Little John. Well, come on, give me the key!"

Robin handed it over, and the man turned to one of the doors. "You don't seem to be defending the vaults very energetically," Robin said.

"Defend, ha!" The man snorted. "That miser sits upstairs with his wine and food, and pays me a pittance while my family is nearly starving. I've been waiting for this for a long time." He opened the door and Robin could see piles of money bags.

"There's only four pack horses," Robin said, trying to estimate the weight.

"They'll only take half of this," the man said. "Of course, you could carry some through the tunnel."

"What tunnel?" Little John asked.

"That one," the man said, pointing to the second door. "It's a siege escape tunnel running out to the woods."

"Are you thinking what I'm thinking?" Robin asked Little John. He called his men. "We'll load the pack horses, and each of you can carry a small amount over your shoulders." The men started loading the pack saddles.

"If someone knocked," Robin asked the guard, "would you open the tunnel door?"

The man smiled wryly. "I'd open it to the devil himself if it would bring about the Sheriff's downfall."

Soon, Little John and 20 men were leading the four horses out of the city, while Robin and the other men left by the tunnel. They were back in the camp before the Sheriff's men had finished uselessly searching the cathedral. Within a few hours, Sir Richard was on his way to London with £800 in gold to secure the King's release.

Prince John Makes His Stand In Nottingham

Several months passed with little activity. Then scouts brought word large bands of armed men were traveling to Nottingham. "Some are Prince John's men," they reported, "but most are strangers."

There were nearly 1,000 fighting men camped in or around the city when a messenger arrived from Sir Richard.

"The King has returned, but Prince John has aroused some barons in the South against him," the man told Robin. "The King has raised an army, and each city has been taken except Nottingham. Prince John is making his last stand here against his brother. Sir Richard will be here with an advance guard in two days."

In that time, Robin received bad news. One of the scouts, Allan a Dale, rushed in to tell Robin Prince John had arrived. "He came in with a large band of soldiers," Allan panted, "and a litter bearing the maid Marian. From the way she was crying, she's a prisoner."

Robin called a meeting of his lieutenants. As they were discussing the situation, Sir Richard and his soldiers arrived.

"The King will be here with the main army tomorrow," Sir Richard said. "He plans to lay siege to the city until Prince John surrenders. I'm to arrange for food and materials for catapults to bombard the city."

"There may be an easier way," Robin said, and told Sir Richard about the tunnel into the castle. "We now have a friend inside. I'd like to get Marian out before she comes to harm."

Sir Richard immediately sent a messenger back to the King. The next morning, the messenger returned, with instructions for Sir Richard to penetrate the castle with 100 men. He was to strike when the King attacked the next dawn.

That day, Robin concentrated on arming his men. They turned in early that night, but were awakened two hours before dawn. Silently, a full hundred of them met Sir Richard's soldiers. They filed through the tunnel to the great door which barred it. Robin lightly knocked. They heard the bolts being released. Then the door opened into the dimly lighted vault room.

The friendly guard was dancing with excitement. "I've been waiting forever. The castle's full of soldiers, and King Richard's men have surrounded the town. What can I do to help?"

Sir Richard asked the man to draw a plan of the castle. As the men crowded around, it was decided that Sir Richard would take 50 men and hold the castle gate, while another 50 would work their way through town to open the main gates to King Richard's men. Robin would occupy the enemy troops in the castle and find Marian.

"If that's the girl locked in the south tower," the friendly guard said, "I'll lead you there."

They waited impatiently until they heard sounds of the attack. A scout reported most of the troops in the castle had been sent out to defend the town wall. Silently, the men streamed out of the cellars into the castle. Within a few minutes, Sir Richard's men had secured the castle gate and were heading for the town gates. Belatedly, the enemy realized they were being attacked.

As Robin and his men fanned throughout the main floor, they met Prince John and some soldiers running to retake the gates. They skidded to a halt when they saw Robin and his heavily armed men.

"You're outnumbered, Prince John," Robin called. "Surrender in the name of King Richard."

"Never!" the treacherous Prince snarled. Swords flashed, and the two groups met in mortal combat. But Robin's men were better trained, so it was all over in a few minutes, except for Robin and the Prince, who found themselves fighting alone in a corner of the main hall.

"Give up," Robin said, forcing the Prince into a corner.

"I should have killed you years ago," the Prince gasped as he rallied. He forced Robin to the hall's great stairs. Step by step, Robin retreated. Then he vaulted over the bannister ten feet to the floor below. The Prince raced down the stairs to meet him.

As they fought, Robin saw his men working around behind the Prince. "No!" he cried. "I'll beat this false Prince myself."

"False Prince?" the noble shouted, "I'll show you who's false," and increased his attack. But, angry, he became careless. Robin caught his blade and spun it out of his hand.

Robin lunged, but stopped with the sword point touching the Prince's chest. "No," he panted. "I'll leave you for your brother's mercy."

Leaving his men to guard the Prince, Robin followed the vault guard to the south tower. There he kicked down a door and released the maid Marian, who rushed into his arms.

"I was so frightened, Robin," she sobbed. "Prince John said he was going to kill King Richard to become King. He said he'd marry me, whether I wanted to or not!"

"I'll never let you go again, Marian," Robin said. "We'll go back to Sherwood, and soon King Richard will take care of Prince John."

They went down to the main hall. Prince John and the Sheriff were under guard. "The King's troops are in the city and fighting toward the castle," Little John reported. "They'll be here soon."

Robin ordered the two captives locked up. Then he led his men back through the tunnel. By the

69

time the King entered the castle unopposed, Robin, Marian and the merry men were back in camp, celebrating the defeat of Prince John and the Sheriff.

The King Meets Robin Hood

King Richard faced a difficult decision. Prince John tried to kill him, but Richard still felt an older brother's affection. Instead of executing or imprisoning his brother, Richard merely asked a promise that John would be loyal. Prince John left for his western estates to lick his wounds.

The Sheriff was a different matter. King Richard removed him from office and sentenced him to five years' imprisonment.

Then King Richard called Richard a Lea. "Sir Richard, I understand Robin Hood and his men subdued the castle and made it possible for you to open the town gates. I would meet this outlaw."

"He's back in Sherwood Forest, your majesty," Sir Richard said. "Robin Hood hasn't been an outlaw since your mother granted him and his men amnesty. He merely protected himself against your enemies. He raised a large part of the money for your ransom, sire."

"I can't believe he's such a paragon," King Richard said. "I'd like to see him when he's acting naturally." The King and Sir Richard put their heads together and came up with a plan to disguise the King, Sir Richard and six loyal nobles as monks.

The next afternoon, sentries found eight monks wandering through Sherwood Forest. They were brought to Robin Hood.

"You're welcome, good fathers," Robin said. "We're celebrating King Richard's victory...and because maid Marian will soon be my bride." He looked lovingly at the pretty girl beside him.

With their cowls pulled over their faces, Robin did not recognize the monks and invited them to enjoy the festivities. There were wrestling matches, which David of Doncaster won. Then Little John and Arthur a Bland took on all comers in quarterstaff jousting, and back to back, fended off all attacks. Finally, it was time for the archery shooting.

Friar Tuck appointed himself contest judge. "Anyone who fails to hit the center of the target shall be eliminated. Anyone who misses the target completely shall get a buffet from my good right arm." There was good natured bantering, but soon the archers started shooting.

One of the first to miss the target completely was Will Scarlet. Friar Tuck felled him with one blow of his mighty arm. After an hour, Little John was declared winner.

"How did you like our contest?" Robin asked the monks.

"Very impressive," King Richard said, "but I've heard Robin Hood is the best archer in all England. I'm disappointed you didn't compete."

Robin jumped up. "Then, good friar, be disappointed no longer." He called for the fine bow Sir Richard a Lea had given him. "I'll put three arrows into the center of the target, no farther apart than a gold crown."

The first arrow flew directly to the center. The second one hit so close it made the first shaft vibrate. Robin smiled at Marian and reached into his quiver for a third arrow. Casually, without seeming to aim, he shot...and completely missed the target!

"A false arrow," Robin cried. "With another, I'll complete the shot." Everyone laughed.

Friar Tuck put his hand on Robin's arm. "No, you must abide by the same rules as the others. You've missed the target, and a buffet you shall get."

Robin smiled ruefully. "If I must, I must, but I claim the privilege of picking who will strike me." He turned to King Richard. "Good father, poor Friar Tuck is weary. Pray do me the honor."

King Richard stood up. "I see Tuck rolled up his sleeve, and so shall I." Robin was surprised to see the muscles on his arm.

Then the King struck, and Robin was lifted off the ground by the blow. He hit the ground again on his back. A mighty shout of laughter went up. Robin shook his head groggily.

"What kind of a monk are you?" he asked. "If I had an army of such monks, I could conquer France." He laughed and climbed to his feet. "I'd like to shake that hand."

One of the other monks pulled back his cowl.

Merry·Robin·
hath·the·
worst·of·
a·
Bargain·

Robin stared. "Sir Richard! What are you doing here?" Then he began to comprehend. He looked searchingly at the large monk. "Are...are you...?"

King Richard pushed back his own cowl, and Robin dropped to one knee. "I've heard many things, both good and bad, about you, Robin Hood. I decided to see for myself what was true."

"Did you decide, your majesty?" Robin asked, smiling up at him.

"One thing," King Richard said, laughing. "Anyone else would still be asleep from that blow, or I grow old without knowing it." He raised Robin to his feet.

"It did rattle my brain a bit," Robin said, wryly. "I'll not ask for a repeat."

The King looked around at the men and their families. "I expected to see a ragtag bunch of outlaws. Instead, I see a well organized, well dressed band who helped me take Nottingham. My mother, Queen Eleanor, granted you all amnesty. I repeat her pardon. You are not outlaws, but freemen of the realm." A mighty cheer went up from the entire group.

Sir Richard a Lea whispered in King Richard's ear. The King waved for quiet, then turned to Robin. "Robert Fitzooth, it's my pleasure to restore your family estates and titles. Henceforth, Robert, Earl of Huntingdon, I shall consider you one of my most faithful barons." Another cheer resounded.

"I must leave soon for the continent, where the King of France is attempting to usurp my family lands. For any who would like to serve me, I offer positions in the ranks of my personal guard."

Then King Richard turned to Will Stutely. "Sir Richard has told me how you organized and managed this camp. I hereby appoint you my representative in Nottinghamshire...Sheriff Stutely." Little John whacked the astounded Stutely on the back

and drove the breath out of him. Everyone laughed and cheered.

Finally, the King looked at Little John. "I've never seen Sherwood Forest before, but if all my forests were this well kept and stocked with game, I'd be the wealthiest monarch in the world. John Little, I appoint you King's Forester, in charge of Sherwood and Barnsdale Forests as long as you shall live."

When the excitement died down, Robin ordered the cooks to bring forth the great feast they had prepared in celebration of King Richard's victory. Now it was also a celebration of their new freedom and new futures.

While they dined, King Richard looked approvingly at the maid Marian. "So Robin Hood intends to marry you. I wish you both a very happy future and hope you have strong sons and lovely daughters." Marian smiled and blushed with happiness. The King suddenly grinned. "I must be here while the accounts of the former Sheriff are being straightened out. Why don't you hold your wedding before I leave, so I can give away the bride?"

And so it happened. Robin Hood — the Earl of Huntingdon — and Marian FitzWater were married in Nottingham's cathedral by Friar Tuck on the first of April, in the fifth year of King Richard the Lion Hearted's reign.

Robin's band and their families filled the cathedral. Will Stutely, Sheriff of Nottingham, and John Little, King's Forester, looked on happily.

After a great reception, attended by the King and all his nobles, the happy couple left for their honeymoon in Huntingdon, which Robin Hood had never seen. And there they lived happily for many a year.